Christmas

Gifts are n...
hold in your hands. The g...
at Christmas is that small baby born in a
stable, though the shepherds and the wise men
did manage to bring presents as well.

These books also celebrate Christmas,
and each deals with a different gift,
the kind that can bring immeasurable love
and contentment down the years—
which we wish for all of you.

Enjoy!

Caroline Anderson's nursing career was brought to an abrupt halt by a back injury, but her interest in medical things led her to work as a medical secretary and then, after completing her teacher training, as a lecturer in Medical Office Practice to trainee medical secretaries. She lives in rural Suffolk with her husband, two daughters, and assorted animals.

Recent titles by the same author:

GIVE ME FOREVER

BY
CAROLINE ANDERSON

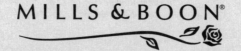

All the characters in this book have no existence outside the imagination of the author, and have no relation whatsoever to anyone bearing the same name or names. They are not even distantly inspired by any individual known or unknown to the author, and all the incidents are pure invention.

*First published in Great Britain 2000
Harlequin Mills & Boon Limited,
Eton House, 18-24 Paradise Road, Richmond, Surrey TW9 1SR*

© Caroline Anderson 2000

ISBN 0 263 82275 3

*Set in Times Roman 10½ on 12 pt.
03-1200-46474*

*Printed and bound in Spain
by Litografia Rosés, S.A., Barcelona*

CHAPTER ONE

HE WAS home.

Mac paused outside the gate for a moment—just sat there in the car with the engine running and let the tension drain away. It had been a long drive, but it was over now. It was all over.

Now he was home, and it felt good. It was late, but the familiar shape of the long low Tudor farmhouse and its barns and stables loomed eerily in the brilliant moonlight. He could see the ice crystals sparkling on the gate and on the grass and shrubs around the house, and thick frost rimed the barn roof and coated the branches of the trees. The moonlight gleamed on the pale cream walls of the house itself and ran in silver diamonds over the leaded windowpanes.

The interior of the house was in darkness, except for one room, the kitchen—his favourite room, the room where all his life they'd laughed and talked and set the world to rights—the room where as a child he'd fed lambs, where his mother fed the whole family, where no one stood on ceremony and everyone was welcome. The light was on, as always, casting a golden stream of welcome onto the gravelled drive, and he could see his mother pottering about—putting the kettle on, probably, for a cup of tea.

Such an ordinary thing to do, but there was a reassuring normality about it that soothed him. He needed soothing. He was feeling raw and brittle and edgy, and a little normality would do him a power of good. He'd missed supper, of course, but that didn't matter. There was always plenty to eat, and he wasn't that hungry—just pleased to be home.

He climbed out of the car and opened the gate, driving through it and triggering the outside lights. The tyres swished over the gravel, and inside the house he heard the dogs bark. The hall light came on and the front door opened to reveal his father standing in the doorway, tall and straight and looking as strong and familiar as ever. He squinted in the bright light of the porch.

'Andrew? Is that you?'

Mac cut the engine and slid out from behind the wheel, straightening slowly. 'Hi.'

The gravel crunched under his father's feet as he strode towards him, a welcoming smile wreathing his face. 'You're home early—we weren't expecting you till the weekend. What a lovely surprise.'

He wasn't the only one who'd been surprised, Mac thought wryly—only his surprise couldn't remotely have been described as 'lovely'.

'They didn't need me, so I decided I might as well get away,' he said, grimly aware of how frugal he was being with the facts. 'It must be the pull of Mum's home cooking.'

'Very likely.' His father engulfed him in a brief hug. 'Good to see you, son.' He stepped back, eyeing him critically, and tutted under his breath. 'You're tired.'

'It's a long way from Cumbria to Suffolk,' Mac reminded him and went to shut the gate to escape those searching eyes.

'I know, but—it's not that sort of tired. You look weary—unhappy.'

Mac shrugged, reaching into the car for his overnight bag. The other things would keep until tomorrow. They'd been packed a little haphazardly—not surprising, under the circumstances.

'I'm fine,' he said lightly. 'Nothing a few hours' sleep won't cure.'

Huh! He wished it was that simple, but it wasn't. Quite apart from the events of today, there was a restlessness, a deep-seated dissatisfaction that was eating away at him. He hadn't settled in the last job, or the one before that, and his personal life—well, his personal life didn't bear thinking about at the moment. Now he'd come home for a while, to look after his father's veterinary practice while his parents took a well-earned rest, and to lick his wounds in private. It would give him time to think about his future, to plan his next, no doubt disastrous, move.

But not now. Now, his mother was coming towards him, arms extended, chiding him for not phoning and warning her so she could cook for him, hugging him against her soft and surprisingly robust little frame, and he forgot his worries and let them lead him inside, into the warmth and security of his old home, where honesty and decency were values that were understood and respected.

The dogs were bouncing around him, butting his hands for attention, too well trained to jump up but not so well trained that they didn't grovel for affection, and he sat down at the kitchen table with their heads on his knees and fondled their ears and let out a huge sigh. 'It's so good to be home,' he said with a smile, and the dogs lashed their tails in agreement.

His parents exchanged a look. It probably spoke volumes, but he was too tired to crack the code. Instead he closed his eyes and just let the familiar scents and sounds surround him.

'Have you eaten?' his mother asked, breaking the silence after a moment. 'There's some casserole left—I could heat it up for you.'

'Sounds good,' he said, suddenly hungry after all. 'I'll just go and change and wash my hands—I feel a bit grubby. I set off as soon as I'd finished operating.' After he'd found Krista and his replacement—

'You'll kill yourself one day, pushing yourself so hard,' she chided gently, and her concerned eyes searched his face, scanning the shadows under his eyes and the lines bracketing his mouth just as his father had done. He knew what she was looking at. He saw it himself every time he looked in the mirror to shave.

He ran a hand over his chin and grimaced. 'I just need a quick spruce. Give me twenty minutes.' He went upstairs to his old room, flung his bag on the bed and pulled out his wash things. The room was chilly as always, but the bathroom next door was over the kitchen and the warmth of the Aga drifted up through the floor and made it cosy.

He stripped off, showered quickly and shaved the stubble off his face. That was better. His mother might give him a minute's peace now. He pulled on clean clothes, jeans and a comfy shirt and a thick sweatshirt over the top, then ran back down to the kitchen just as his mother set a plate of steaming stew on the table.

'Eat,' she said firmly, and he didn't bother to argue. Suddenly he was ravenously hungry, and his stomach growled in anticipation.

They didn't talk, just sat quietly until he'd finished, then as he pushed the empty plate away his mother put a cup of coffee down beside him and smiled. 'Better?'

'Much. Thanks.' He wrapped an arm round her hips and hugged her, and she leant against him with a sigh and hugged him back.

'It's so good to have you home. We've missed you,' she said.

'I've missed you, too. How are things? Anything going on?'

The phone rang, and his father gave a wry laugh. 'Yes—I'm on call. What's new?' He stood up and reached for the phone, jotting notes and speaking in terse monosyllables for a moment. 'Right, I'll be with you shortly. Have some hot water ready to warm the paraffin, if you can, please.'

He hung up. 'Horse with colic. I might be hours. Jenny, can you contact me on the mobile if there's anyone else needing me?'

'I could take your calls till you're back,' Mac offered.

'We'll see,' his father said. 'You need to rest.'

'Not that badly. There's always tomorrow—'

The phone rang again, and his father scooped up the receiver. 'McWilliam.' His brow furrowed, and then he raised a brow at his son. 'Fine. Someone will be with you shortly. Leave an outside light on, could you?'

He cradled the phone. 'One of Mrs Blewitt's dogs has passed out while he was chasing the cat. Might be a heart problem. Would you do me a favour and go and see it?'

Mac stood up with alacrity, only too glad to get away from the searching glances his mother was still giving him and the grilling he knew was just seconds away. 'Sure. I like old Mrs Blewitt. I'll go and see the dog. No doubt it's hugely overweight.'

'No doubt,' his father agreed blandly. 'You know the way—Clematis Cottage?'

Mac nodded, then his father was gone, out of the door and away to the horse with colic. Mac kissed his mother goodbye, pulled on his coat and went out with a sigh of relief. He couldn't run from the truth forever, but this would give him tonight, at least, to collect his thoughts...

He could remember Mrs Blewitt's cottage. It was down a lane in the village, set slightly apart from the others, a little tumbledown but very quaint. He could also remember a stream of overweight cats and dogs being brought to the surgery over the years, all killed with kindness.

She'll never learn, he thought with a smile.

He drove through the familiar roads of the village where he'd grown up with a sense of quiet relief. Time to reflect, he thought. This village, so familiar, so reliable, so much home, was just what he needed.

He pulled up outside the cottage, took his bag from the back of the Discovery and opened the rickety gate. Immediately there was a chorus of high-pitched and furious little barks, and he was poised with his hand over the knocker when the door swung inwards and a woman looked up at him—a young, beautiful woman with a smile that was too wide and eyes that could light up the sky. Eyes that were so familiar he knew them as well as he knew his own.

His hand dropped unheeded to his side. 'Ruth?'

For a stunned second they stared at each other, then her smile widened and she gave a small, incredulous little laugh. 'Mac?'

He felt her laugh right down to his bones, and the shards of ice inside him began to melt in the warmth of her smile.

'I can't believe it's you!' With a laugh of delight he dropped his bag, swept her up into his arms and hugged her hard. Then he set her down, stood back at arm's length and looked down at her.

'Oh, it's so good to see you!' he said with a choked laugh, and hugged her again.

Ruth Walker, he thought with a surge of happiness, and felt the ice melt a little more. Coming home was getting better and better...

He's grown, she thought inconsequentially. Not taller—of course not—but more solid. His chest was deeper, his arms thicker, his shoulders broader. He was a man now, of course, no longer the lanky boy she'd grown up with, but his smile still lit up his eyes and warmed her heart, as it always had.

She stepped back and dragged him inside, pushing the door shut with her hip and smiling up at him in genuine delight. 'I might have known—your father sounded a bit vague on the phone. I should have smelled a rat, but you weren't due home yet!'

He chuckled. 'I had no idea you were here, he didn't warn me at all. I suppose you're on duty—is Mrs Blewitt ill?'

She felt her smile fade. 'Ah. You don't know.

Mac, she's dead—she died months ago,' she said gently. 'I'm living here now.'

His brow pleated in a puzzled frown. 'But—my father said one of her dogs—'

Ruth sighed. 'It's complicated. Come in. Toby's in the kitchen. He keeps walking round in circles, and he's got his head at a funny angle. And he's hugely fat, before you bother to tell me. He's on a diet but I think he can live on fresh air. Either that or he's scavenging from somewhere.'

She led him through to the kitchen and crouched down by the old oil-fired cooker. The dogs' basket was beside it, in a space under the worktop out of draughts and in the warmth. It was the only really cosy place in the whole cottage, and there had been times in the past few weeks when Ruth had considered cuddling up in there with the little dogs instead of going upstairs to sleep.

She stroked him gently on his shoulder. 'Here, Toby, Mac's come to see you. Say hello.'

The dog lifted an eyebrow and his tail flickered slightly once.

'Poor old boy. What's the matter, then?' Mac crooned, crouching down beside her and holding out his hand for the dog to sniff.

It seemed suddenly far too crowded, and as their thighs brushed she was instantly and totally aware of every inch of his well-built, muscular body so close to hers. How strange. She stood up and moved away, filling the kettle automatically while she puzzled over her reaction. 'Coffee?' she offered in a slightly strained voice, but he didn't seem to notice.

'Thanks,' he murmured absently, running his

hands over the dog. 'How long's he been like this? My father said something about him chasing a cat.'

'He was. One minute he was fine, the next there was a thud and he was out cold.'

She propped her hips against the cupboards opposite and watched him as he listened to the dog's heart and lungs, then checked his eyes with an ophthalmoscope. His shoulders had never been so broad, surely—

'Did you say a thud?'

Ruth nodded. 'Yes—well, sort of. Why?'

'I'm just wondering if he could have banged his head. Was he near anything? A chair leg or something like that? He's got cataracts—he might not have seen it, and he does seem to have a little bump on his head.'

Ruth thought back to the incident. 'Maybe. His sight is dodgy—yes, it's quite possible. He fell over right by the little gateleg table. I thought he fell against it, but he might easily have run into it instead.'

'Will he let me pick him up?'

'Oh, yes. He'll let anybody pick him up. He's a softie.'

She watched as Mac lifted the fat little dog out of his bed and put him on his feet. He wobbled for a moment, then steadied up.

'Can you call him? I want to see him walk.'

Ruth crouched down and held out her hand. 'Toby? Come here, sweetheart,' she called encouragingly, and he staggered towards her, veering off to the right. His head was still held at a funny angle, and she could tell he was disorientated and—concussed?

'Good boy,' she murmured, going to Toby and stroking him as a reward for his effort. 'Has he got concussion?'

Mac nodded. 'I think so. Hopefully it's nothing more long-lasting, but I think you need to watch him. I don't think he needs to come into the surgery for observation overnight, you can keep a better eye on him here, but perhaps in the morning if he's still bad you should bring him over.'

'I'm off duty tomorrow—I can stay with him whatever,' she explained.

Mac nodded, tucking the dog back into his bed and stroking him gently. 'Good. I think he just needs to rest. And don't feed him for a few hours. Not that it will hurt him—he's well overweight. What are you feeding him on?'

Ruth laughed. 'Not much. The same as the others—a small-bite mixer and tinned food in gravy. I cut them all down drastically when I inherited them, but he's taking ages to lose it.'

Mac lifted his head and looked up at her, his eyes an astonishing blue in the gloomy kitchen. They really were the most beautiful colour—

'Inherited?' he said.

She sighed again. 'It's a long story. How do you take your coffee?'

'White, no sugar, not too strong. I'd like to stay for a while and keep him under observation, if that's OK? If I'm not happy we'll have him in for assessment for a few days but, hopefully, as I say, it won't be necessary.'

'Do you think he could need treatment?' she asked as she made the coffee. 'A scan or something? I mean, there's money there for it—whatever he needs, even if it's a brain tumour or something. Mrs Blewitt made sure of that.'

Mac studied her oddly. 'OK. We'll see, but I'd be reluctant to send him off to Cambridge for an operation, for instance. He's an old dog, and he might have a heart valve disorder—it's quite common in Yorkshire terriers. I can hear a bit of a murmur, I think, but the stove's gurgling a bit so it's hard to tell. We'll do X-rays and an ECG at the surgery, but I think you've got to accept that he's an old dog, Ruth.'

His voice was gentle, but there was no mistaking his message. 'He's going blind,' he went on, 'and he's too overweight to be a good anaesthetic risk if he has got a tumour, even assuming it's operable. At the moment I'm almost sure it's just concussion, but if I should turn out to be wrong I'd be inclined to let things take their course.'

Ruth nodded. He was right, of course. Just because the money was there didn't mean the animals had to be kept alive at all costs, and in truth even if it was a tumour he was happy enough curled up on her lap or by the stove, and as long as he was, she thought, she should let him carry on without any interference. If only she could get him thinner...

'He's not suffering any pain, is he?' she asked Mac, just checking to be sure. 'I mean—he is fat and not swollen with something insidious?'

'No.' He straightened and grinned. 'He'll just hate you when you cut his food down again. He'll need a special low-calorie diet, but it's expensive,' he warned.

'That's fine, it's what the money's for.'

He looked puzzled, and she gave a soft laugh.

'Mrs Blewitt left me her cottage and some money to look after the animals for the rest of their lives. I had no idea until she died.'

He gave a low whistle. 'Wow. I bet her relatives were thrilled.'

She pulled a face, remembering the almighty rows that had ensued. 'Not very. Her second cousin was the nearest relation, and he threatened me with court action, but it was all tied up legally and there was nothing he could do. She'd taken care of that—she'd told the solicitor her cousin wasn't in the slightest bit interested in her when she was alive, and her animals needed their home and were much more important than him. I believe he handed her views on verbatim.'

Mac chuckled. 'I bet that went down like a lead balloon.'

'Oh, absolutely. I'm not sure I was that thrilled, either, but I'd promised her I'd make sure they were all right when she died, so I don't have a choice, although I'd had in mind finding them good homes. Apparently we weren't on the same wavelength!'

He winced and grinned. 'Apparently not. Can you cope?'

'Yes, I suppose so,' she said with a tired little laugh. 'They're all right. There are just rather a lot of them.'

'How many?'

She pulled a face. 'Three dogs—Toby and his sister Twinkle, and a Cairn terrier called Dougal that looks like a grubby floor mop—and seven cats. Oh, and the budgie.'

'Seven cats and a budgie? Ouch.'

She laughed again. 'Don't. I live in fear of coming in and finding a little heap of feathers. Still, it entertains the cats, and the cats entertain the dogs. Come and sit down—the fire's lit, but it doesn't draw very well. I must get the chimney swept.'

He followed her through to the sitting room, ducking under the low doorway and dwarfing the little room with his presence. Had he always seemed that big, or was it just in the close confines of the small cottage and under the low ceiling? She threw another log on the fire and waved to a chair, scolding Twinkle and Dougal for jumping up at him.

'Kick the cat off and have a seat, if you don't mind the hairs. Dougal, stop it!'

He laughed. 'Occupational hazard. Why do you think people in the country wear tweed instead of plain colours?' He scooped the cat up, sat down and settled it on his lap, then made room for Dougal as well beside his leg. 'So, you inherited the cottage and enough money to look after the animals for life,' he said, absently fondling Dougal's ear.

'That's right. Knowing where to draw the line is what's difficult. Do I do what Mrs B would have done, or what's right and fair for the animals? I'm not sure they're one and the same, always.'

His lips pursed thoughtfully. 'That's a hard call. I think you have to do what's right for the animals and hope she'd understand. Your own conscience needs to be clear.'

She smiled in relief. 'I'm so glad to hear you say that. It's what I feel, but I know I'll be racked with guilt when I have to make that final decision for one of them. Thank God we don't have to make those decisions for our families!'

'Absolutely. Animals are much easier—you can be fair and kind without having the law after you.'

'Do you believe in euthanasia?' she asked curiously, wanting to know more about the Mac he was now.

He looked thoughtful. 'For people? I don't know. I practise it all the time on animals for very sound reasons—and it makes life a whole heck of a lot tidier. I'm not sure if that would be good or bad in the case of humans. The jury's still out. I know I draw the line at treating everything we can just because we can, regardless of what it does to the lives of those involved. Sometimes I think we preserve a beating heart and call it saving a life. I find that hard to justify.'

Ruth nodded slowly. 'I agree. Thank goodness I don't have to make those sorts of decisions for my patients—just this lot.'

He trailed a hand over the ginger cat and threw her a smile of understanding. 'So what happens when they've all died of old age or whatever? Does the cottage go to charity or the cousin, or is it yours?'

'Mine.' She was curled up in the other chair, Toby's sister Twinkle on her lap, and she stroked her thoughtfully. 'Although I have to say it's a bit of a gift horse. It needs rewiring, there's no central heating and the windows all leak like sieves. It's going to cost me a fortune that I don't have to bring it up to date—starting next week with the electricians. That's why I've got tomorrow off, because they're coming to finalise what I want and tell me what they'll need access to. Then at least I'll dare put on some heaters without worrying about blowing the fuses.'

He rolled his eyes. 'What a legacy.'

'Indeed.' She gave a wry chuckle. 'Whatever. So, enough about me—tell me what you're doing here. Your father said you were coming home at Christmas for a while, but it's still November.'

'Only just,' he pointed out, and she flapped a hand at his argument.

'Whatever. It's still going to be a long Christmas break. How can you afford to leave your job for so long?'

He said nothing for an age, just sat there scratching the cat's ears and enduring the flexing of her claws in his leg, the silence broken only by the hissing of the log on the fire and the contented purring of the cat. For a while she thought he wouldn't answer and wondered if she'd floundered into forbidden territory, then he lifted his head and met her eyes, and she knew she had.

'I've finished there,' he said flatly, and she realised he wasn't just talking about the job. 'I—It wasn't working. My personal life was a mess, my job satisfaction was nil—it was time to move on.'

Ruth's curiosity was thoroughly aroused, but he wasn't inviting questions. She could see the lines around his mouth that hadn't been there all those years ago, the shadows under his eyes, and in his eyes themselves a sort of defeat that troubled her soft heart and made her want to reach out to him.

She gave a silent sigh. She never had known when to butt out, but he needed a friend, and that was something she'd always been to him. She couldn't stop now—not when he needed her.

'Who was she?' she asked softly.

Mac's hand stilled. To his credit he didn't pretend not to understand. Instead he gave a bitter smile and looked away, his eyes haunted.

'One of the partners—another vet. She was older than me—thirty-two or so. She latched onto me when I arrived, and within weeks we were involved in an affair. It wasn't entirely successful. We used to fight a lot, but then we'd make up and it would all settle down again—till the next time. It got very wearing.'

'Were you engaged?'

He shook his head. 'No. We didn't talk about the future—we weren't really stable enough to have one, and I don't think either of us was interested in permanence, but we drifted on for nearly two years in a strangely unsatisfactory on-off relationship. We never even lived together—not officially. Not properly. It was—vaguer than that.'

He stopped, and she waited for a moment, then jogged him gently. 'So what happened? What changed?'

He shrugged. 'It wasn't working. None of it was working. I didn't like the job—I didn't feel I was given enough responsibility, and the senior partner did all the surgery at his insistence. It would have been all right if he hadn't been useless, but I've seen that same surgery done by experts in their field, and I knew he was messing things up that should have been straightforward. Things I could have done better. Animals were dying that should have lived, and he was ripping people off. I was more than ready to leave the job.'

'And the woman?'

'Krista? We were going nowhere either, so I told her it was over, handed in my notice and they interviewed my replacement. He started on Monday— the idea being I spent a few days handing over to him.'

His voice was getting tight, and she could see a muscle working in his jaw. She sensed he was about to clam up, so she pushed him again, just gently, like before. 'What happened, Mac?'

For a moment she thought he wouldn't answer, that he'd refuse to tell her the punchline. She wouldn't have minded. She had a feeling she didn't want to hear his answer, but then he lifted his head and met her eyes, and they were blazing with anger.

'I was operating this lunchtime,' he said flatly. 'We finished off, and everyone went down to the pub because one of the nurses had a birthday. I stayed and cleared up, and then I heard noises in one of the consulting rooms. I went in to check— we keep drugs and syringes in the rooms, needles, that sort of thing, and we have to be careful because of drug users. Anyway, I went in—and—there they were...'

'Together?' she queried, shocked. 'I mean—like that?'

He looked away, his jaw working furiously. 'Yes. Very definitely *together*. They were so engrossed they didn't even hear me, till I slammed the door behind me. She ran after me, apologising, grovelling, but I just—I wanted to get out. I told them he clearly didn't need any pointers from me in following in my footsteps, he seemed to be more than happy in my shoes, but I felt he might have waited for them to cool before he put them on.'

'That was restrained,' she said with a wry smile. 'I think I would have put his teeth down his throat.'

He gave a harsh cough of laughter. 'Oh, no. I was closer to hitting her. He was just another victim. I doubt if she'd bothered to tell him anything about us—not that there was an "us" by this stage, but I still think she might have had the decency to wait until I'd left, or at least be a little circumspect. Anyway, I drove to the pub, had a quick drink with them, said I was leaving and packed and went. End of conversation.'

She was silent for a moment, giving him time to get his anger back in check, and then she stood up and went over to him, placing a gentle hand on his shoulder. 'I'm sorry,' she said quietly. 'That must have been hard, loving her.'

'I didn't,' he said honestly. 'I never loved her. We were just scratching the same itch. It just pees me off that she was so blatant—so indiscreet. I expected more from her, but that's the story of my life. Nothing, no one, ever lives up to my expectations, but I was rather shocked that I could have made such a grave error of judgement in ever getting involved with her.'

Ruth perched on the arm of his chair and searched his eyes. The anger was gone now, replaced by a deep sadness and disappointment, and she felt a lump in her throat. There was nothing she could say, so she said nothing, just squeezed his shoulder in silent support.

His hand came up and covered hers, their fingers twining, and he closed his eyes, his jaw working again. 'Am I just an idealist?' he asked after a moment, frustration echoing in his voice. 'Is it a flaw in me that I look for too much in people?'

'I don't think expecting decency and fidelity and honesty in a relationship is asking for too much,' she told him frankly. 'I think you're right to be angry. I'd be angry. I'd be angry with both of them.'

'Thanks. That helps.'

'So what will you do now?' she asked after a moment.

He shrugged. 'I don't know. Cover for my father while he and my mother go on this world tour, and think, I suppose. Empty my mind and wait to see what fills it.'

She nodded, understanding absolutely what he was talking about. There were times when you had to let go of things that weren't working, to move on and see what took their place. She wondered what time would reveal for Mac, and whether he would tell her.

She was glad he'd been able to tell her this much—and glad she'd been there for him. He'd needed to get it off his chest, but it wasn't something he could easily talk to his parents about.

Still, she'd been there, by chance, and he'd talked to her, and she was touched that he still felt able to open up to her. They'd been good friends—not that close, really, not as close as she might have liked, but probably close enough for her sanity. He had a way with the girls—or had had, as a younger man. Now, at twenty-eight or so, that lazy charm was probably even more lethal when he turned it on.

Still, she knew him well enough to ignore it. He didn't mean it, he just seemed to exude charm like other people breathed air. It seemed almost invol-

untary, as natural to him as breathing, and the very
naturalness of it was a huge part of his very great
appeal.

To her, at least. She stood up, needing space, and
threw him a smile. 'Another coffee?'

'Yes—and I ought to check Toby.' He stood up
and followed her into the kitchen, then hesitated for
a moment. 'Look, Ruth—I'm sorry about all that. I
don't usually unburden like that, but I just needed
to talk.'

She smiled up at him and reached up, patting his
chest comfortingly. 'You ought to do it more often—it's good for you.'

For a moment their eyes locked, and her heart
flopped against her ribs, and then he looked away,
crouching down to check Toby, and her heart re-
sumed its normal rhythm.

What a fool, she thought. He's just a friend. I
must be going mad. They chatted for a while longer,
Mac asking her questions about the village and its
inhabitants, and she talked and watched him unwind
and enjoyed his company as she hadn't enjoyed anyone's for years.

Then, with one last quick check on the dog, he
pulled on his coat and paused at the door.

'Thanks,' he said quietly. 'I'm sorry you got the
flak.'

She hugged him without thinking. 'Don't worry,
I'm used to it. Listening's what I do best.'

He hugged her back, and then he bent his head
and brushed her cheek with his lips, and fire shim-
mered over her skin.

Again, she thought. I'm reacting to him again. I need to get out more.

Then he smiled and opened the door and was gone, and the house seemed empty without him.

CHAPTER TWO

TOBY was still a bit rickety on his legs the next day, but he seemed a little better, so Ruth rang Mac and told him, and spent the day quietly at home showing the electricians round and discussing what would need moving before they could come in and do the wiring.

The place was going to be in absolute chaos, but they promised to keep the disruption to a minimum, and she knew they'd look after the animals and make sure no harm came to them.

The following day, Friday, she was back at work, and it seemed all anyone could talk about was Mac.

'Young Andy McWilliam is back,' Mrs Frayne said when Ruth went to change her ulcer dressing. 'Such a good-looking boy, I always thought. I wonder what he's like now.'

Even better, Ruth thought, and tried to pay attention to her job and not think of Mac's eyes or his broad shoulders filling the gap beside the stove as he bent over the dog, or the casual, friendly kiss he'd dropped on her cheek as he'd left that had kept her awake half the night, thinking about the slight scrape of his beard against her skin, the scent of soap and man that had teased her nostrils, the firm pressure of his hand on her shoulder as he'd squeezed it in farewell.

'Ruth?'

She blinked, startled. 'Sorry, Mrs Frayne—I was miles away. Did you say something?'

She gave a wheezy chuckle. 'Thinking about that young man, were you? Can't say I blame you. If I was thirty years younger I'd be thinking about him. I nearly got a dog once as an excuse to see his father! He's another good-looking devil.'

Ruth laughed and pressed the four-layer dressing firmly in place. 'You're a wicked woman—what about your husband?'

'Oh, I'm only joking, dear. I loved my husband, and he loved me—but it didn't stop him finding excuses to go to the village shop when Helen was there!'

Ruth laughed dutifully, and then hastily packed up her bits and pieces, gathered all the dirty dressings together and put them in a sealed clinical waste bag and bid farewell to Mrs Frayne before the woman could say anything else about Mac.

Not that it made any difference where she went.

'You and young McWilliam were good friends once, weren't you?' Mr Hubbard, the ex-publican, said when she went to check his catheter. 'I can remember you all in the pub on Saturday nights—a rowdy lot you were, if I remember correctly.'

'I'm sure you do,' Ruth admitted with a laugh. 'That was the Young Farmers—always rowdy.'

'I always thought you had a soft spot for him—the way you used to look at him.'

She gave an awkward smile. 'No—not Mac. He was always in love with someone else.'

'And never you, eh? Never mind, dear. The others are all gone or married now—perhaps it's your turn.'

'Oh, I don't think so,' she denied quickly, ignoring the quiver of something that could just possibly have been hope. 'We're still just friends.'

'If you say so,' he said, having the last word as ever. Ruth kept her mouth shut. There didn't seem to be any point in talking about it. Everyone had their own opinion, and hers was clearly going to be disregarded.

'I think you're right, you might have a bit of a urinary infection,' Ruth told him, changing the subject and studying the cloudy, murky contents of the little bottle she held in her hand.

'Looks like scrumpy cider,' he said, peering at it. 'Thought it was a bit odd, and I did feel hot and cold.'

Ruth nodded. 'You've got a little bit of a raised temperature. Anyway, I've taken this sample from the tube, and we'll send it off for testing. I'll get Dr Carter to come and see you later today. All right?'

'Thank you, dear,' he said, smiling fondly. 'How are all Mrs Blewitt's creatures?'

'Oh, not too bad,' she said, crossing her fingers.

'Pity. You want one of them to go sick so you can take it to see young Andrew—nothing like bringing yourself to his attention to make him notice you.'

'We're just friends,' she repeated firmly, not mentioning Toby and his bang on the head, and packed up and left.

Was it just coincidence, or did Mr Hubbard have a hotline to Cupid? Toby was fine when she got home, but one of the cats came in holding a front paw off the ground, and she could see blood on it.

'Let me see, Thomas,' she coaxed, but Thomas was having none of it. As an expression of his appreciation he slashed her with his other front paw, then limped off into the sitting room and proceeded to bleed freely on the only decent cushion.

Damn. It was all Mr Hubbard's fault, she thought, and rang the practice.

'Mr McWilliam is tied up in surgery with an emergency,' she was told, 'and the other vets have all gone. You could bring him in and wait, but it may be some time.'

'Oh, dear. Um, I've got a cat with a cut paw— it's bleeding quite freely. You couldn't ask him what I should do, could you? The cat won't let me put pressure on it.'

'Hang on.' The girl vanished for ages, then came back. 'He said ring his home—his son will look at it for you. OK?'

'Sure. I'll do that.'

She thanked the receptionist and rang off, chewed her lip for a second and studied the steady spread of the bloodstain on her best cushion. There was no help for it. With a sigh she picked up the phone again and punched in the number of the McWilliams' house.

Mac answered, his voice deep and gruff and much too sexy for her peace of mind.

'It's Ruth,' she said, and quickly explained about the cat. 'I hate to trouble you, but your father's busy and he suggested I ring you. I'm sorry to be a nuisance—'

'Not a problem. I'm on my own here this afternoon, so I could do with the company. Bring it straight to the house, can you? We've got a little surgery here—I can probably look at it and sew it up if necessary without bothering to go to the main surgery. Come round to the side door, I'll leave the light on.'

She thanked him, seized the ungrateful cat and thrust him, clawing and yowling, into the cat carrier, then drove to the house. Mac was waiting for her, and within minutes he'd restrained Thomas, given him a mild sedative, pulled a nasty shard of glass out of his paw, washed it and bound it up.

'It won't need stitches,' he told her. 'Just antibiotics. Can you get pills into him?'

She laughed without humour. 'Only if he's dead.'

The smile nearly wiped her legs out from under her. 'OK. He can have injections. Much easier. I'll drop by and do it each evening. OK?'

'Fine,' she said, wondering if he'd always been so darned good-looking or if he'd got better as he'd got older. Her stomach, not interested in the aesthetics of the situation, rumbled loudly and he chuckled.

'Have you eaten?' he asked.

Ruth shook her head. 'No. No time. I got in and found the cat bleeding all over the place. Food was the last thing on my mind.'

He smiled again, that wonderful megawatt smile that crinkled his eyes and made her heart flip-flop. 'Let's drop the cat at home and go to the pub—like old times,' he suggested, and she wondered if Mr Hubbard really did have that hotline or if, for once, God was on her side.

'I need to feed all the animals, and they've been on their own all day,' she said with the last remnant of her common sense, 'quite apart from which I could do with getting out of my uniform.'

'Why don't I pick you up in an hour, then? That would give you time to fuss them all a bit, and I can do my father's stock to save him time later. Deal?'

She couldn't resist him. She didn't even bother to try, because there was no point. She didn't want to resist—and anyway, resist what? A quick bar snack and a drink in the local with a man she'd known most of her life? Hardly the last word in Great Romances, was it?

'Deal,' she said, and, picking up the disgruntled and sleepy Thomas, she posted him into the cat carrier and went home, humming all the way.

They were delighted to see her, the dogs bouncing round her feet, the cats winding round her legs and milling around on the worktops and yammering at her for food. As fast as she put them down, they were back on again, and she gave up and resigned herself to dying of something ghastly.

It took her five minutes to feed the animals and check that they were all OK while she wiped up Thomas's blood and put the cushion cover to soak in cold water. Thomas seemed fine, no worse for his ordeal if rather woozy and disgusted, but she was slightly worried about Toby, who seemed to be off his food a little.

'Are you still feeling sickly, love?' she asked him gently, scratching behind his ears, and he leant into her hand and whimpered with ecstasy.

He seemed all right. He seemed perfectly fine, in fact, not a thing wrong with him apart from the loss of appetite. How odd. Still, he was fine, and time was running away with her.

She ran upstairs into the freezing bedroom, sorted through her clothes and stopped herself choosing a skirt and pretty top.

'It's a quick drink in the local!' she chided herself, and put out a pair of jeans and a lambswool roll-neck in a pretty soft lilac that showed off her dark hair and contrasted interestingly with her green eyes. It was comfy, she wore it often and it was just coincidence, she told herself, that she looked better in it than in most things in her wardrobe!

She couldn't shower—there wasn't one in the primitive little cottage—but the water was hot and she bathed and dried at lightning speed in the chilly bathroom downstairs, ran back up and pulled on her clothes before her slightly damp skin made her freeze to death.

Just the second the rewiring was done she was having storage heaters everywhere, she vowed, and blow the running expenses. She was sick of being cold. She went down to the kitchen to do her make-up, and had one eye on and one off when she heard the knocker.

She contemplated leaving it, but then a familiar voice called through the letter box and she went and let Mac in, grumbling gently at him for being early.

He trailed her into the kitchen. 'Thought I'd come and check on my patients,' he said, crouching down and fussing the animals. 'The stock didn't take as long as I thought they would. How's Toby?'

'Fine,' she said, and then paused, mascara wand in hand. 'Well—he's off his food, but he still seems fine. I'm not sure.' She peered into the mirror and whisked the mascara over her eyelashes, then watched Mac in the mirror as he ran his hands over the little dog.

'He certainly looks fine,' Mac agreed. Toby didn't bother to contradict them. He was too busy sniffing Mac's legs for interesting smells. 'How's the cat?' Mac added, glancing up at her in the mirror.

She laughed and dropped the mascara back onto the window-sill. 'Sulking. He's gone off in a huff—he's on my bed. I expect he'll spend the evening getting the bandage off and then bleed all over my quilt cover.'

'Sounds par for the course,' he said with a chuckle. 'That's only what I'd expect.' He straightened up and smiled at her. 'All fixed?'

'Yup. I'll just get the dogs in.' She called Twinkle in from the garden, locked the back door and patted them all goodbye, then snagged her coat from the banisters at the bottom of the stairs.

'Here, let me,' he said, and held the coat for her, tucking it solicitously around her shoulders and sending a shiver of awareness through her.

Not that it was reciprocated, she thought in irritation with herself. He hadn't even made a socially polite comment on how she looked! Oh, well. Just a drink and a bite in the pub with an old friend, she reminded herself. Why are you trying to turn it into something else?

It was a lovely evening. They bumped into Julie and Mike Foster in the bar, and ended up sharing a table and rehashing old times. They'd been part of the original group, and had married when Julie had come back from university six years before. Ruth had seen them around, of course, and they'd met up at village functions from time to time, but they were tied up with each other and their children and the farm, and didn't go out much.

Ruth guessed that this was a rare treat for them, and all the more fun for Mac's company. It was strange, she thought, how his very presence made the jokes funnier and the mood lighter, but, then, it always had.

It was quite busy, being a Friday night, and after they'd eaten Julie and Mike invited them back to their farm. 'We've got to let the babysitter go home, so we can't be too late, but it seems a shame to break up the party. Why don't you come back?' Mike coaxed. 'Just for a while.'

'I'm on duty tomorrow,' Ruth said regretfully.

Mike shrugged. 'That's all right. I can't be too late because I'm milking at five. Just a coffee.'

So they went back and had just a coffee, followed by just another one, and then she noticed Mike yawning and caught Mac's eye. He nodded, and they said their goodbyes and left, agreeing that they should do it again soon. It was only a few minutes to her cottage, and he pulled up outside and cut the engine, turning to look at her in the cold, eerie light of the moon.

'Coffee?' she offered automatically, but he shook his head.

'No. You're tired, and, anyway, I don't want to go in too late and disturb my parents. My father's looking very tired these days and it's been a long week.'

She nodded. 'OK.' She smiled across at him, wishing—oh, wishing all sorts of things. Things she couldn't have. Things that were silly and based on reactions that were entirely inappropriate. Remember that woman—Krista, was it, the faithless hussy? Remember he's on the rebound. Remember you're just friends, that's all. 'Mac, thanks for this evening, it's been lovely,' she said quietly, reaching for the doorhandle.

He looked thoughtful, but he didn't say anything, just slid out from behind the wheel and walked her up the path. At the door he paused, searching her eyes in the moonlight, and then he smiled, a fleeting quirk of his lips.

'Goodnight, Ruth,' he said softly, and, bending, he pressed a quick, meaningless kiss to her lips.

Meaningless. Friendly. Totally asexual.

She stood there transfixed, rooted to the spot as he strode away up the path, climbed into the Discovery and slammed the door. He paused, watching her, and on autopilot she slid her key in the lock, turned it and went in, closing the door behind her.

Seconds later she heard the engine fire, and then he pulled away, turning into her drive and then going back towards his home, the clatter of the diesel engine fading into the night.

The dogs greeted her like a long-lost friend, and she fussed and cuddled them, stroked the cats, chatted to the budgie through the bars of his cage and then went into the kitchen to make a drink. Despite her protestations about an early night, there was no way she'd sleep after that kiss.

Harmless though it had been, it had rocked her on her foundations, and she needed time to think, time to put it all back into perspective and remind herself that it was meaningless and platonic and she was overreacting.

A little after midnight she gave up and went to bed, no nearer to understanding her response to him, and certainly no nearer to dealing with it. She spent the night with Thomas alternately purring in her ear and biting at his bandage, and at six o'clock she gave up, got up and washed and dressed herself and took the dogs for a walk.

Her first call that morning was to a new patient, John Grainger, just discharged from hospital following the placement of a permanent catheter into his abdominal wall so that he could have peritoneal dialysis. He worked from home, and was unable to devote the time necessary to go to hospital for haemodialysis two or three times a week.

He'd decided to opt for CAPD, continuous ambulatory peritoneal dialysis, which meant that several times a day he would have to drain the fluid out of his abdominal cavity and replace it with fresh dialysate to cleanse his blood.

Ruth's job was to assess how he was coping, make sure he was carrying out the procedures in a safe and aseptic way and that there were no problems that he hadn't reported.

His wife answered the door, a sweet but rather harassed woman in her forties, and she led Ruth through to the sitting room. 'He's in here, having a rest. He's still feeling a little weary after all the upheaval,' she explained.

'I'm sure,' Ruth agreed, and hurried to his side before he struggled up to greet her. 'Don't get up, you don't want to stand on ceremony with me,' she said with a reassuring smile, and held out her hand.

'I'm Ruth, and you must be John. I'm the community nurse and I'm going to be making sure you're happy with what you have to do and that you're managing all right. How did you get on this morning first thing, or haven't you tried yet?'

He pulled a face. 'I don't know. It seems harder at home—I ran out of hands! I was doing all right at the hospital, but I had to ask Linda to help me, just to have enough fingers to do the job! Sometimes I wonder if I've done the right thing.'

'I'm sure you have. You'll have much more freedom like this.'

He gave a weary laugh. 'Except I feel like a balloon filled with water half the time.'

'Well,' she said practically, 'if you find it doesn't work for you, you can always go back to the haemodialysis unit and be linked up to the kidney machines again.'

He nodded thoughtfully, and Ruth quickly checked that everything seemed all right with the catheter, the little tube that had been inserted into his abdominal wall beside his navel. The site was clean and pink and healthy, so, reassured that there was no infection, she then went through the technique of changing the fluid with him, just to make sure he was doing it correctly.

It was most important that the connector on the end of the tube wasn't contaminated, and that the tube coming from the bags was similarly clean, or he could easily end up with peritonitis, potentially life-threatening and certainly not good news for the dialysis.

She checked the yellow fluid that drained out for quantity and colour, and also for clarity. 'You do know if you get little stringy bits in the effluent you have to let me know, don't you? It looks a bit like jellyfish. It's called fibrin—it's a totally harmless substance, but it can clog the catheter and mess things up, and we just put heparin in the bags for a few changes to dissolve it, so I need to know.'

He nodded. 'OK. Sure.'

'And if you get any shortness of breath, swollen ankles, puffy hands, that sort of thing, you need to tell me—it's just about fluid balance, really, and I'll be here every day for a while to make sure everything's going well.'

She left him then, happy that he understood the importance of the sterile routine and confident that, given time, he'd be happier with what he had to do. The important thing was that he had his freedom now, and would be able to work more efficiently.

Her next call was to Mr Hubbard to check his catheter again and see how he was doing. The doctor had called the day before and put him on antibiotics for his urinary infection, and Ruth had to make sure he was starting to improve and that his urine didn't contain anything of concern. He'd had a slight temperature, as well, and she was a little worried.

She needn't have been. She found him improved already, and in excellent spirits.

Too excellent.

'Hear you were out at the pub last night with young McWilliam,' he said smugly.

'Didn't take you long, considering you don't get out now, did it?' she said with mock indignation.

He grinned, totally unabashed. 'Took my advice, then.'

'What?'

'Had a problem with the cat, I hear.'

'Yes, I stuck a piece of glass in his foot on purpose,' she said a little tartly, exasperated. 'And did you also hear that we met up with Julie and Mike Foster and went back for coffee to their farm?' she added, scanning the urine in the bag as she emptied it and measured the amount.

'That was nice,' he said mildly, totally unfazed by her manner. 'How does it look?'

'Like urine, which is good news. Yesterday, as you said, it looked like scrumpy cider—cloudy and full of bits. The antibiotic must be working well already.'

'And I've been drinking more. The doc told me I must. I'd cut down a bit because it's such a nuisance having to empty and measure the bag all the time.'

'It can't take much longer than just having a pee,' she chided. 'You have to drink plenty, you know that. I've told you and told you—'

'Oh, don't nag me, girl. I know that. I was just feeling lazy.'

'Well, get all your friends that keep popping in with nothing better to do but gossip about my private life to make you a drink—you should get several cups a day without having to lift a finger!' she told him a little sharply, and then spoiled it by smiling. 'You'll be all right now. I'll see you in a few days. Call if you've got a problem.'

She let herself out, finished her calls and checked into the surgery again to see if there were any other calls she had to make.

'I think you're done for the day,' Tom Carter told her with a smile. 'Unlike me—I've got several people coming in for an emergency surgery in a few minutes, and a string of calls. Looks like a busy weekend brewing.'

'Shout if you need me,' Ruth said sympathetically, and went home to her brood. Thomas had managed to get his bandage off and was lying in the middle of her bed in a pile of shredded gauze and tape, licking his paw industriously. He let her look at it, and it seemed to have healed almost completely.

'What a clever cat,' she murmured, scooping up all the mess and putting it in the bin. 'How did you get so clever?'

'Mreow,' he squawked, and stood up and stretched, arching his back and purring at her.

'You can't be hungry,' she chided. 'You've probably eaten half a mile of tape. Just don't need an operation, all right, or Mr Hubbard will get suspicious.'

She scooped him up and carried him down to the kitchen, and found Toby busily being sick.

'Oh, sweetheart!' she cried, and cleared up, studying the evidence with confusion. 'What have you been eating? I'm sure I didn't give you anything that looked like that.'

He cocked his head on one side and whined at her.

She looked at him curiously. 'Are you scavenging?' she asked.

He ran to the door, and she let him out into the garden and watched him as he was sick again. Later he developed diarrhoea, but she was determined not to take him to Mac. Not now—not on Saturday evening! Mr Hubbard would have a field day!

And then she remembered he was coming anyway

to give Thomas his antibiotic injection, and her heart did a silly little skitter. She was contemplating the inside of her fridge when the doorbell rang, and she straightened her jumper, checked her hair in the mirror and winced, shoved the loose strands back out of the way and opened the door.

'Hi,' he said, his mouth twisted into a wry smile. 'Is this a good time?'

'Fine. Come in, I'll put the kettle on.'

'That would be nice. How are they all?'

'Toby's chucking up and he's got a touch of the runs, but Thomas seems as fit as a flea.'

'Still got the bandage on?'

She laughed. 'Not quite. He spent the morning on my bed shredding it into a million pieces. He was terribly pleased with himself when I got home.'

Mac chuckled and followed her into the little kitchen. Toby was lying in his bed looking bloated and unhappy, and Mac frowned at him. 'You look a bit rough, little mate. What's happened to you?' he crooned, and crouched down beside him.

The little stump of tail wiggled slightly and he licked Mac's hand just once.

'Oh, you are feeling sorry for yourself,' he murmured, gently prodding his abdomen. 'I think you've been a bit of a pig, actually. You've got a very full tummy.'

'I wondered if he was eating the remains of dead rabbits or something, but I don't see how he can be. He can't get out of the garden.'

Mac laughed. 'I wouldn't be too sure. He's not big. I reckon if you go round the garden carefully you'll find a little gap just big enough for him to squeeze through. I think he's taking himself off for little snacks, aren't you, son?'

Toby looked as if butter wouldn't melt in his mouth, and Ruth snorted with disgust. 'I wondered why he wasn't losing weight—I'll have to check the fence in the morning.' She hovered, the fridge door open for the milk, and looked at him. 'Fancy something to eat?' she asked as casually as she could manage, but he shook his head.

'Sorry—I'd love to, but Mum's cooking. I've got a better idea,' he added without pause for thought. 'Why don't you join us? It wouldn't be the first time, and there's bound to be enough. My mother doesn't know the meaning of moderation.'

Ruth chuckled, remembering the groaning table from her adolescence. 'Are you sure? You ought to check with her.'

'It's fine,' he promised.

'I'll only come if you ask her,' she insisted, so he rang, and his mother said something that made him laugh.

'She's delighted—she said you're the only one who ever said thank you after a meal, and you're welcome any time.'

'Oh—I'm sure I'm not,' she said, pleased by his words and glad she'd left a good impression. Somehow it seemed to matter rather a lot...

'You ought to give Thomas his injection—he's in the sitting room, I think, on the cushion with the stain on it. I couldn't get it all out.'

'Typical. They never bleed on things that don't matter. Right, young Thomas, let's be having you.'

He was back seconds later, the cat injected, and looked at her expectantly. 'Shall we go, then?'

She looked down at herself. 'Oh—don't I need to change? I'm just in my scruffing-around clothes.'

'And we're not? Don't dress up or we'll all feel self-conscious.'

So she went, and they had a wonderful meal, and all the way through it she could feel Mrs McWilliam studying them speculatively. Ruth had the strangest feeling that she was pleased they'd met up again, and wondered—just idly, just in passing—if the invitation for supper had been her idea.

Whatever. She didn't care whose idea it had been. It was lovely to be back there, just like old times.

'They say you can't turn the clock back, but I really feel we have,' she said with a laugh as they cleared the table. 'I don't feel any different to when I was seventeen. The last ten years seem to have slipped away without my permission, somehow.'

'I know the feeling,' Jenny said fervently. 'I'm worried about Bill. He's getting more and more tired—he's sixty now, and I think he should give up. Maybe now Andrew's home.'

'I thought he was only here for Christmas?' Ruth said, puzzled.

'Oh, he is—well, until the end of January. We're going away for six weeks to see Alec in Australia, as you know. But if he gets on well with the practice…'

She left the words hanging, and there was no time to say more because Mac and his father came back into the room. They made coffee and took it through to the drawing room by the woodburner, and Ruth mulled Jenny's words over in her head and finished the sentence.

If he gets on well with the practice—maybe he'll stay?

Now that was a thought worth considering…

CHAPTER THREE

THE following morning Ruth lay in bed and thought longingly of the time when she could have a lie-in on her days off. Not now, though. Now she could hear the animals in the kitchen underneath, little yips and whines and scratching noises, and pitiful, starving mews from the cats.

'Anybody would think you were never fed,' she grumbled, and, pulling on her dressing-gown and slipper-socks, she padded downstairs and opened the door.

She was greeted with ecstasy. The dogs jumped up, the cats wound round her legs and yammered— the noise was horrendous. 'Why did I say I'd do this?' she asked them plaintively, carefully measuring out dog food. 'I must have been mad. You should have gone to the RSPCA, the lot of you.'

The cats mewed impatiently, but finally they were all fed and she filled the kettle, put it on the Rayburn and slumped against the worktop to watch them eat.

Then she straightened up and looked round, suddenly realising that someone was missing. 'Toby? Toby, where are you?'

She opened the back door and looked around, but there was no sign of the little dog. Where could he be? All of them, dogs included, used the cat flap to get in and out, but he was always there for food.

'Toby? Toby-Toby-Toby!' she called, but there was nothing.

With a sick feeling of dread, she checked the other rooms in the house, and ran upstairs to pull on her jeans and a good thick sweater. It was bitterly cold despite the sun, and she was worried that he was trapped somewhere or lying injured. She ran down, pulled on her boots and coat and ran out into the garden, checking under the shrubs for any sign of him.

There was nothing, but there was no way he could have got into the road, because the side gate was firmly shut as ever. Mac might be right, she thought, there could be a hole in the fence. She checked every inch, calling Toby repeatedly, and then finally she found what she was looking for—a hole, not much more than a shallow depression under the edge of the wire mesh, with a clear trail leading from it.

And on the other side of the fence was a field, let out to pasture with cows and horses grazing on it. Ruth climbed over the fence and ran over the field, calling him desperately, more than ever convinced that something dreadful must have happened to him.

He never missed his breakfast—his supper, yes, but never his breakfast. Her imagination, too fertile for her own good, started creating hideous scenarios that did nothing for her peace of mind. She stopped running aimlessly about and forced herself to be rational.

Where would he be? Where could he have gone? She scanned the valley, looking over the fields for other houses, places where he might have gone to scavenge food, perhaps.

Her nearest neighbour was across the field, but they were away this weekend, or so she understood from Mrs Frayne, fount of all gossip. Still, it might be worth a check…

She ran down the field diagonally, and as she drew level with the hedge she could hear whimpering sounds coming from the house.

'Toby?'

A thin, tired yip greeted her, and she pushed through a hole in the hedge and ran to the back of the house, following the sound of his crying.

And there, half in, half out of the cat flap, was her dog, stuck fast, his face tragic in its delight at seeing her.

'Oh, Toby, you silly boy! How did you do that?' she asked.

There was a cat sitting on a plant pot nearby, looking indignant and hungry, and Ruth guessed that, like Winnie-the-Pooh in Rabbit's house, Toby had gone in, eaten all the cat's food and then got stuck on the way out. Would he, like Pooh, have to stay there until he was thin enough to emerge? When were they due back?

He cried again, and she noticed that his sides were raw where he'd struggled to free himself.

She hesitated for a moment, then stroked him one last time and stood up. 'Stay here, little one. I'll be back,' she promised, and squirmed through the hole in the hedge, ran like the wind across the field and let herself back in through her back door.

With shaking fingers she dialled Mac's home number, and nearly cried with relief when he answered. 'Mac, Toby's stuck in next door's cat flap and they're away—I don't know what to do!'

'I'll come. Stay there, I'll be with you in two minutes.'

It was three, but she didn't care. She'd locked the back door, locked the cat flap and trapped them all inside by the time he arrived, and she ran out, still breathless, and climbed in beside him.

'Where to?' he asked, and she pointed down the road. She was too puffed to speak, but he understood, and seconds later they'd pulled up outside the other cottage.

'Right, where is he?' he asked, jumping out, and with the last vestige of strength in her horribly unfit legs, she ran round the back and pointed to the dog.

'There,' she gasped, and Mac crouched down and scratched Toby's ears, talking softly to him while she recovered.

'He's cold—he must have been here for hours,' he said. 'When did you miss him?'

'This morning—about half an hour ago, I suppose. I gave them all breakfast, but he wasn't there. He's never been missing before, but I found the hole in the fence and eventually heard him.'

Mac examined the dog as well as he could, then sat back on his heels. 'I think we're going to have to take out the cat flap,' he said. 'Is there any way you can contact your neighbours?'

Ruth shook her head. 'No—none. I don't have a mobile number for them, and I don't know where they've gone. I might be able to find out, but it could take hours.'

He shook his head. 'No good. We have to get him out quickly. He's getting distressed and I don't like the look of him—he's finding it hard to breathe properly, and his heart isn't strong. We'll just have to make it right with them when they get back.'

He stood up. 'I'll get a screwdriver from the car—stay with him.'

She knelt down and stroked Toby, and he whimpered and sagged against her. 'Poor boy,' she crooned, and wondered how long it could take Mac to find a screwdriver.

He was back in a few moments, but it seemed an age. 'I've brought one or two other things, like some lubricant. Right, let's have a look.'

The screws were rusty, of course, but with a massive effort he turned them and the two halves separated. They were no further forward, though, because the dog was still firmly stuck in both halves, and they couldn't free him, even with the lubricating jelly. There was nothing to pull against.

'Damn,' Mac muttered, shifting backwards to get a better look. He knocked into a pot and it rolled over.

And there, on the ground, was a key. For the door?

'Geronimo!' Mac said, twisting it in the lock and swinging the door carefully open. There was a mess on the floor behind the little dog where he had relieved himself, either in desperation or in fright, but at least now they could get at both ends. With a great deal of tugging and squirming and pushing, they managed to get the outside part of the cat-flap frame away from his head end, and then he slipped easily through the door and they were able to lay him down on the mat and work the inside part of the frame off over his head as well.

'Good grief, dog, however much did you eat?' Mac asked, gently feeling his tummy. There was a bowl beside the water dish—a bowl that would have

held more than enough food for the cat for days—
and it was licked clean.

'You naughty boy,' Ruth chided despairingly.
'Look at you!'

'His sides are pretty bruised and raw, and his
chest is very sore. What a sorry little dog.' Mac
listened to his heart. 'Seems all right. His lungs are
a bit wheezy, but that's probably all the whining and
the constriction.'

He looked round and wrinkled his nose. 'Right,
we need to rebuild the cat flap, clear up the floor
and feed their cat—and then we could do with leaving them a note to explain. Are they good neighbours?'

Ruth gave a slightly hysterical laugh. 'I don't
know, but I think we're just about to find out—I can
hear a car on the drive.'

'Perhaps we'd better intercept them before they
find the place trashed,' he said with a smile. 'You
stay here, I'll tell them.'

He left her clearing up the mess, and a few moments later the couple appeared at the back door,
delighted to see that the dog was all right, sorry that
they'd been away and only too relieved that nothing
really nasty had happened.

'At least we now know who is pinching all our
cat food!' the woman joked, stroking the disgruntled
cat and reassuring him.

'Well, it won't happen again,' Ruth promised. 'I
can't believe he'd be stupid enough to try it, but I'm
going home now to mend the fence, and young Toby
here's going on a serious diet!'

They offered to clear up the mess, but were ushered out to go and look after the dog and not to worry.

Ruth couldn't imagine what Mac had said to them, but it seemed to have done the trick. More evidence of that abundant charm! she thought wryly.

They drove back to her cottage, and she put Toby out in the garden for a few minutes while they blocked up his escape route and checked that the rest of the fence was secure. He was sick again, but otherwise seemed simply sorry for himself and crept into his warm bed to sleep it off.

'I'll give him some cream to put on his scrapes, but otherwise he should be all right,' Mac said with a smile.

'Thank you so much,' Ruth said fervently. 'What do I owe you?'

He looked stunned. 'Owe me? Nothing! Don't be silly.'

'But I must—'

'Put the kettle on. I'll let you give me a coffee— I was just about to drink mine when you rang.'

She felt guilty, but there was no point in insulting him, and after all, she supposed, he'd done little that any other friend wouldn't have done. She chewed her lip and contemplated her reasons for calling him, and didn't have to go very far before she came up against the answer.

She'd wanted his help. Not just anyone's, but his. Oh, she could justify it because he was a vet and Toby was a dog, but that wasn't the real reason and, if she wasn't going to delude herself completely, she had to admit it.

'Want me to light the fire in here?' he offered from the sitting room.

She followed him in and found him inspecting Thomas's paw. 'I doubt if you can—it's got worse and worse. I'm going to have to have it swept.'

'Don't do that—I'll get the rods from home. Have you got an old sheet?'

Ruth laughed. 'I've got nothing but. I'm sure I can find one that's even worse than the others.'

'Right, you dig that out, I'll get the rods. Back in a tick.'

'But your coffee—'

'Later. Let's get the place warmed up a bit.'

The door banged behind him, and she looked down into the two mugs on the worktop. 'Later, he says.' She opened the fridge. She could just about run to three or four rounds of cheese on toast—unless his mother was going to cook Sunday lunch.

Oh, well. She'd wait and ask him when he got back. In the meantime she opened the airing cupboard in the corner of the kitchen and removed two of the cats who'd taken advantage of the broken catch, then sorted through the sheets.

'That should do,' she said with satisfaction, and wedged the door shut with a little bit of paper to keep the cats out. Then, armed with her dust-sheet, she went through to the sitting room and cleared away the furniture, rolled back the tired and tatty carpet and cleared out the grate.

By the time she'd finished he was back, sensibly clad in overalls and gloves, and he quickly and efficiently screwed the rods together one at a time and pushed them up the chimney.

'It's getting heavy,' he warned. 'I think you'll be amazed at the amount of soot we get out. I should stand back if I were you.'

She heeded his warning, and carefully, without disturbing the edge of the sheet, he withdrew the rods. Suddenly there was a great rush and a huge cloud of soot burst through the bottom of the sheet and billowed across the room.

She closed her eyes briefly, then ran for more sheets to cover the furniture. A little soot she'd bargained on—but this!

He repeated the process three times before he got to the top of the chimney, and then he scooped the soot into a bin bag and carried it carefully outside while Ruth wiped ineffectually at the hideous mess.

'Let me,' he offered, and within minutes he'd cleared it up, at least to the point where a damp cloth stood a chance. She brought a bucket of hot water and wiped and rinsed repeatedly for ages, then finally the colour of the tiles reappeared.

He'd swept and vacuumed the floor, and then they rolled the carpet back, rearranged the furniture and stood back.

'Coffee?' she offered.

Mac gave a sexy, lopsided grin. 'Coffee? I think I need a stiff brandy after that lot. How about lunch in the pub?'

'We're filthy!' she exclaimed, but he laughed.

'Wash—it comes off. I've got my clothes here, I'll just have to rinse in the sink if that's OK.'

Then, to her utter amazement and confusion, he stripped off his overalls and stood there in her kitchen in socks and the sexiest snug-fitting briefs she'd ever seen, sluicing water over his head and humming softly.

He peered at her under his arm, and waved her

away. 'Come on, hurry up, we'll be too late for lunch if you don't move.'

She went, too stunned to argue, and bathed at lightning speed, her mind filled with images of his lean, sleek muscles rippling under the pale gold of his skin.

Since when had he looked like that? She remembered swimming parties in the summer, with a lanky youth who'd been all skin and bone and muscle—but it hadn't done this to her. It hadn't turn her insides to fire and made her heart beat like a steam hammer.

She dressed in the cold, damp bathroom—anything rather than go out there in her dressing-gown and feel so naked and vulnerable while he was out there looking like that—

'Come on!' he called, banging on the door.

She opened it, to find him fully dressed. How disappointing. 'What about Toby?' she asked with the last of her common sense.

'He's fine. I've just checked him. Come on, I'm starving and dying of thirst.'

He towed her out of the door, slotted her into the car and drove to the pub without once—quite—breaking the speed limit. They were too late for hot food, but the landlady promised to make them some sandwiches, and they sat in the corner with alcohol-free lager and grinned.

'So much for your brandy,' Ruth teased.

He chuckled. 'I don't need spirits, I've got you,' he said with a wickedly sexy wink, and her heart flip-flopped while her mouth came out with a sassy retort all by itself.

Was he going to start to flirt with her?

And if so, did this mean that he'd noticed her, as well? He'd never given her any indication that she was attractive to him. Was that for the same reason that she'd said nothing to him?

She gave up. It was all too complicated. Their sandwiches came and she put the intricacies of their relationship out of her mind and concentrated on her food.

It was only later, when he dropped her back at her house and checked Toby again, that she thought of it. They were standing in the kitchen, and he reached out a strong, blunt fingertip and stroked it across her face.

'You've got a smut on you,' he murmured, and she wasn't sure if she'd imagined it or if his voice really was low and sexy, like dark chocolate.

She backed away. 'Where?' she asked, and looked in the mirror. There was nothing there— nothing except confusion and anticipation in her eyes. 'I can't see anything.'

'It's gone. How about lighting the fire and seeing if it's worked?' he suggested, and she met his eyes in the mirror.

'Um—we could. I was going to stack all the furniture up and roll up the carpet later, but it would be nice if it was warm in the house, and I expect the electricians would appreciate a fire.'

It took him a very few moments, and the flames were drawing away, licking through the kindling and setting the logs alight. He sat back on his heels and looked up at her in satisfaction. 'There you are—Superman strikes again.'

'In your dreams,' she said dampeningly, and went to make tea. Anything rather than look at the denim of his jeans straining taut over the powerful muscles of his thighs, or the twinkle in his eye, or the quirk in those full, firm lips—

'Oh, by the way, Mum said would you like to come for supper? It's a roast—the last one. They leave on Tuesday.'

'So soon?'

'Yes—I'm going to have to spend tomorrow at the surgery. Just think, this is my last day of freedom and decent food.'

He appeared in the sitting-room doorway, propping up the frame with those broad shoulders, long legs crossed casually at the ankle, looking too sexy for his own good.

Or hers.

'So, will you come?'

She blinked and collected herself. 'What—? Oh, supper. Um, yes, that would be lovely,' she agreed, too weak to resist.

It was the story of her life these days. How odd, when until now she'd been so much in control of every thought or action...

Typical! Just when she'd wanted to be independent, her car wouldn't start!

She rang Mac. 'It just groans,' she said disgustedly. 'It won't even turn over, let alone fire. I'm not going to be able to come for supper. I'll have to call out the breakdown service and wait until they arrive, because I need it tomorrow. I'll have to have a new battery.'

'I'll come. Don't worry, I can probably get it fixed, or we might have a battery here that will do the job.'

So yet again, for the third time that day, he came to her rescue. Talk about a knight in shining armour, she thought wearily. She'd have to find someone else to call on, it was getting ridiculous!

'Hold this,' he said, handing her a big, heavy torch. He peered under her car's bonnet, grunted something unintelligible as he pulled the leads off her battery terminals and scrubbed them with a wire brush, then connected them back up again. 'Try now,' he said, all of three minutes after he'd arrived, and the darned thing started first time.

'Corroded connections,' he announced smugly. 'Shouldn't be a problem any more. Got any petroleum jelly?'

'Vaseline?'

'That's the stuff.'

'No.'

He rolled his eyes. 'Follow me, I'll put some on at home. We don't have time to hang around—the Yorkshires were just going in the oven when I left.'

She needed no urging. Jenny McWilliam's Yorkshire puddings were legendary. They set off in convoy, once she'd checked all the animals and had made sure that the bloated and self-pitying Toby didn't need to go out yet again.

It was dark, of course, but the wind had picked up and there was squally rain falling now that made it seem even darker. The roads were slippery, so she hung back and gave Mac a little more room than usual.

It was just as well she did because, as they drove through the dip in the bottom of the village, he hit the brakes and skidded to a halt.

A car careered up the bank opposite and rolled

over, just as she slithered to a halt behind Mac, and she jumped out of the car and ran across the road.

It was only then that she heard the horse screaming, and in Mac's headlights saw what she'd missed before. A big, dark horse was rearing up, lashing out with its hooves, and then suddenly it seemed to free itself from whatever it was attached to and galloped into the stable yard.

Mac ran towards where it had been, and she saw him kneel beside a huddled figure—the rider? No, the horse had had no tack on. Someone leading it?

She looked at the car on its roof, and saw that the people inside were crawling out of the windows.

'Are you all OK?' she asked, helping them to their feet.

A girl was crying, but one of the boys assured her they were all right. They were young, only just old enough to drive, she guessed, and probably very shaken.

'Did we hit it?' a lad asked, probably the driver.

'I don't know, I didn't see,' she confessed. 'Come over into the light, let's get a look at you. Mac, is everything OK?'

'Injured hand. How about the occupants of the car?'

'Fine, I think,' she told him, hurrying to his side. 'What about the horse?'

'He's up and moving—that's probably a good sign. Could you take over from me and hold this pressure point while I get my torch and dressings kit? I want to stop the bleeding if I can.'

She knelt down on the muddy verge and put her fingers over his, smiling at the woman and talking softly to her to reassure her. She looked pale and strained and she was obviously shocked. Ruth looked at her hand, and swallowed an exclamation. Small wonder! Two of her fingers were hanging at a very odd angle, and one of them seemed almost detached. Oddly, the woman didn't complain of any pain, but often severe traumatic injuries like hers didn't hurt for a while because the nerves went into shock.

'I've phoned for the police and ambulances,' Mac told her as he returned. 'Could you move your car back and park it up the hill a little with hazard flashers on? I'll get these covered and see if I can stop the bleeding, and we should have some help by then.'

'These fingers need splinting and elevating,' she warned, and he nodded.

'I know. I'll do it—I've got tongue depressors to strap them to.'

'What about Ted?' the woman asked weakly.

'Ted?'

'My horse.'

'I think he's all right,' Mac said soothingly. 'He's gone into the stable yard. I'll go and check in a minute. Just let me wrap you up a bit and make the area safe, and we'll get him sorted out. Is there anyone we can call? Anyone in the house?'

She shook her head. 'No. Find him,' she pleaded. 'I'm so worried. You need to call a vet—'

'I'm a vet. Trust me, he's all right. He's up and moving. He'll keep. You won't.'

Ruth left him reasoning with her as he worked, and moved her car to try and prevent any more accidents. Then she checked the youngsters from the overturned car. One seemed to have a nasty cut on her head that was streaming blood, another had a possible fracture of the forearm.

She found a roll of cotton wool sandwiched in gauze in the back of the Discovery and covered the cut with a chunk of it, taping it roughly over the girl's hair, and improvised a sling for the boy with the arm out of a length of crêpe bandage.

They were all lucky to be alive, though, she thought shakily. The horse, the owner, the kids from the car—all of them had had a narrow escape.

She heard a siren in the distance, and moments later the police were there sorting out the mercifully light traffic, checking that no fuel was leaking from the upturned car, asking questions about what had happened.

Ruth still wasn't sure, but gradually it emerged that the kids had come out of a side turning, and in the lights from Mac's car they hadn't seen the horse approaching from the other direction. By the time they had, it had been too late to avoid it, and the wing mirror had struck the horse, just before the car had mounted the bank and rolled over.

And the woman's fingers, Ruth realised, must have been tangled in the lead rope. Ouch.

She left the police dealing with the youngsters and went back to their patient. She was looking very shocked, and Mac was threatening to put a line in and give her some IV fluids when the first ambulance arrived.

She was whisked away, still fretting about her horse, and, as the other ambulance had arrived by then, Ruth went with Mac into the stable yard to look for him.

'I'm worried about him—it was only a glancing

blow, but he might be bleeding. I want to find him and check him over quickly but, I warn you, it may not be nice.'

'You said he was up and moving and all right.'

He snorted and shook his head, scanning the yard with his torch. 'I've seen a horse galloping with one hoof hanging by a flap of skin—it didn't seem to notice until it stopped, and then it just fell over. He could be in a real state. Here—this looks likely.'

They found him cowering in the back of his stable, shaking and sweating and rolling his eyes, and Mac soothed him gently, approaching him with great calm. It took about five minutes to remove his New Zealand rug, and then they got their first proper look at him.

'He's got a nasty cut on his side—can you shine the torch on it, but mind his eyes? I don't want him spooked. He's resting that leg, as well,' he added as the light from the torch swept over the horse. 'Damn. Looks like a fracture.'

'Is that very bad? Will you have to put him down?'

'Depends—she might have insurance, or it might be nothing much. Some fractures heal easily, others are impossible. It might have to go to Newmarket, if she can afford it. There's a wonderful equine surgical unit there.'

Whoa-ing and soothing and talking gibberish, he slid his hand back over the horse's flank and touched the point of the hip. The horse snorted and backed away, favouring the leg heavily, and Mac shook his head.

'Fractured iliac crest, I think,' he murmured. 'The cut needs stitching, but the hip will need weeks of box rest, at least. I'll have to sedate him to stitch this—I think I need my father's help. We might have to prop him up. I don't want him going down out of control, he might not get up again. I'll call him.'

He pulled out his mobile phone, punched in the number and spoke briefly to his father. A few minutes later Bill arrived, and between them they sedated the horse, stitched the long slash in his side and spread arnica cream over the whole area.

'He'll need a deeper bed—Ruth, can you see if you can find another bale of straw somewhere? In a barn or something?' Mac's father asked as they held the horse upright with sheer brute strength. She went out with a torch and scouted around, finally locating the straw in a shut stable.

She shook it out, built up good thick banks around the walls and then checked the hay and water.

Both seemed fresh, as they'd expected, as the horse had been coming in for the night. They'd reversed the sedative after giving an injection of pain relief, and the horse gradually steadied up and took his own weight so he was no longer leaning against them. They watched him for a few minutes, and when he reached out and pulled a mouthful of hay from his hay net, Mac and his father exchanged a smile.

'He'll do. I'll come back later,' Mac said. 'Do you know the owner's name?'

'Lucy Kennedy—she's a client,' Mac's father told him. 'I'll ring the hospital. Come on, we'd better go home if the police have finished with the two of you, or Jenny will feed the beef to the dogs.'

Ruth nodded, and started to walk towards her car, but her legs suddenly seemed weak and unhelpful.

'You OK?' Mac asked softly.

She shivered, aware for the first time that it was raining steadily and that she was soaked and frozen. 'It was all so sudden. I feel a bit shocked.'

'Me, too. I thought for sure it was going to be much, much worse. Come on, let's go home.' He put his arm round her and led her to her car, then looked at her closely. 'Are you all right to drive?'

She summoned a smile. 'I'll manage. It's only a little way.'

'Just think of the Yorkshires waiting,' he said with an encouraging wink, and she laughed.

'You always say the right thing,' she replied, and felt her legs steady.

'I'll see you at home,' he said, and helped her into the car.

Home, she thought wistfully. Since her father had walked out on them fifteen years ago and her mother had later remarried a younger man with a family, she'd felt she hadn't really had a home any more. Granted, she had the cottage, but it was Mrs Blewitt's cottage, not hers, really, and there was no way it was home.

But Mac's—now that was home, a real family home, with warmth and love and laughter and a welcome for everyone.

It sounded good. It sounded more than good, in fact, it sounded wonderful, and she could hardly wait to get there.

CHAPTER FOUR

JENNY MCWILLIAM was waiting for them, and took
one look at Ruth and ushered her upstairs to change
into clean clothes. She found some jeans, a little on
the loose side but quite wearable, and gave her a
thick rugby shirt of Mac's because her jumper was
bloodstained and messy around the cuffs.

'That should keep you warm enough—I'll put
your things in a bag for you,' she said with a smile.
'Have a quick wash—I'll get the supper on the
table.'

Ruth was downstairs five minutes later, her face
and hands thoroughly scrubbed and feeling pink and
shiny. It's a good job I'm not trying to seduce Mac,
she thought with a wry laugh as she caught sight of
herself in the mirror.

They were all in the kitchen, talking over the
events of the evening, and when she went in Mac
looked up and smiled a welcome. 'Hi. Feeling better?' he asked gently, and she nodded.

'I was just cold and wet as much as anything.'

'It's a thoroughly nasty night now,' Jenny said.
'It's a good job you found your little dog, or he
would have been miserable.'

Ruth flashed a guilty look at Mac. 'Do you suppose he's all right? I didn't intend to be out so long.'

'He's fine. He's sleeping. Relax. We can go back
after supper and check him, if you like.'

She sighed. 'I just feel so responsible. I mean,

they aren't mine! It's like looking after somebody else's demented granny, looking after that lot. They're all ancient—well, most of them, and I just feel so...'

'Responsible?' Mac repeated with a grin. 'Why didn't you just say no?'

'And let her down? Besides, the cousin was obnoxious—he would have had all the animals put down and sold the house to a builder. He didn't deserve it. She loved that little house.'

'You are such a softie,' Jenny said with a kindly smile. 'I reckon she left them all to you because she knew you'd do just what you're doing.'

'What, torturing myself over them?' She chuckled. 'I expect I'll get used to it.'

'Oh, you will,' Bill agreed. 'After the first few accidents and emergencies, you get quite philosophical, don't you, Jen?'

'Don't,' she groaned, and they laughed and moved to the table.

The food was wonderful, none the worse for having been kept waiting, and Ruth found she was ravenous. The sandwich in the pub was hours ago, and the adrenaline surge of the accident had used up tons of fuel, or so it seemed.

She had a second helping, then tucked into homemade trifle running with thick double cream from the farm down the lane and layered with wonderful home-grown fruit from the freezer.

By the end she felt like Toby, but fortunately she wasn't stuck in a cat flap. Instead she curled up by the woodburner, sipped a delicious cup of coffee and listened with one ear to their plans for Australia.

They were off on Tuesday morning, and Mac was

driving them to the airport with their luggage. It sounded like a long flight, and she didn't envy them. She found it difficult to sit still for a couple of hours, never mind twenty-odd.

She glanced at her watch, and a pang of guilt assailed her again.

'I'm sorry, I'm going to have to go and check the dog,' she said in a lull. 'I do hope you have a wonderful time—it sounds really exciting.'

'It is. I'm sure it's going to be fantastic, and it will be so good to see Alec again.'

'Give him my best, won't you?' Ruth said, and kissed Jenny's cheek. 'Thank you so much for a lovely evening—yet again. I'll have to return the favour when you get home. It's time I started entertaining. Maybe by then my wiring'll work and I'll be able to have the kettle and the lights on at the same time without blowing all the fuses!'

They laughed, and Bill said, 'We'll hold you to that.'

'Don't get over-excited, I'm not much of a cook,' Ruth warned, and slipped her damp coat on. Jenny handed her the carrier bag with her clothes in, and then to her surprise Mac reached for his coat.

'I'll follow you. I need to give Thomas his injection, I forgot it earlier, and I can check Toby and reassure you so you can get some sleep.'

'There's no need,' she protested, but he held up his hand.

'Just humour me, please?'

Ruth gave in. Apart from anything else, she was more than happy to have his company for a little longer.

They drove back through the wet and stormy

night, past the place where the accident had happened. Apart from the odd sparkle from broken glass, there was no trace left of the drama that had been enacted there, and it gave it all a surreal quality.

They went in to find the dog was fine, as Mac had assured her, and she felt silly for worrying. And now she'd broken up the evening and he was going to go any second—

'I'll get the fire going again—or aren't I invited for coffee?' Mac said, propping up her kitchen wall and giving her a lopsided grin.

'Of course you're invited,' she chided, her heart singing because he was going to stay after all and not just check the animals and leave. She found him in the sitting room with the injected Thomas on his lap, and Toby sprawled, still bloated, in front of the cheerful, crackling fire.

'It's a good job you've got a spark guard, because that fire's drawing so well now that the wood's spitting furiously. You ought to get seasoned wood—it sparks less.'

'I was just using up what was in the shed. I expect it was free from a neighbour or something.'

'Probably. Mrs Blewitt was very careful with her money. Nobody realised she had any.'

'She saved it all so her animals could be looked after when she died. Silly old thing, she was permanently frozen and hungry to keep them. It was really touching.'

'And unusual. It makes a change to hear about responsible pet ownership. There are some really callous bastards out there who have no business keeping animals.'

She shooed the dogs off her chair onto the floor, and Dougal hopped back up onto her lap the moment she sat down and claimed her.

'This lot are just spoilt to death,' she said disgustedly.

'I can see how much you hate them,' he teased, and then added, 'Your electricians come in the morning, don't they? Do you have to clear anything up?'

A cold chill ran over her. 'Oh, blast, I'd forgotten! Yes, I do—I have to get this carpet up from under the furniture, and sort out the bedrooms a bit. Not that there's much, but I think they're going to have to work round some of it. There simply isn't room to move everything out of the way, the house is too small.'

'I'll help you,' he offered, and when they'd finished their coffee they shifted what they could in the sitting room, then went upstairs.

The small bedroom was all right, tidy and fairly bare, and the rug was easy to roll up and remove.

Her bedroom, however, was a totally different kettle of fish. For a start, it was dominated by a double bed in the middle of the long wall, and it was quite clear that she'd climbed out of it this morning and left it in a tangled heap.

'I usually make it,' she said, dragging up the quilt with an embarrassed laugh. 'This morning was a bit chaotic, though.'

'I'll forgive you,' Mac said with a lazy, sexy smile, and suddenly the bed seemed even bigger and dreadfully symbolic.

'Um—the carpet,' she said, flustered, and he lifted the end of the bed while she pulled the carpet out from beneath it. They rolled it, stood it up in the corner and dusted off their hands.

'That the lot?' he asked, and she nodded.

'Yes—thanks. You'd better get back to your parents—I expect there are a million things you need to ask your father.'

He shook his head. 'I can ask one of the vets if I get stuck, but I wouldn't mind getting back just to spend time with them. I've hardly seen them for years and they're off the day after tomorrow. Besides, you're tired. You've had a hell of a day.'

'And I've involved you in just about every moment of it when you could have been with them,' she said guiltily. 'I'm sorry.'

'Don't apologise. Just look after yourself, keep the spark guard over the front of the fire and don't let the animals out of your sight!'

She laughed, and then there was a silence, a strange silence that seemed to cry out for something, but what?

A kiss?

The bed behind her seemed to grow suddenly, and she ushered him down the stairs as if they were about to catch fire.

As they reached the bottom there was a gust of wind and a crash, and she sighed. 'That's another slate. You'd better go,' she said, thrusting his coat at him. 'The weather's getting worse. Drive carefully.'

'Always do,' he vowed. Pulling on his coat, he bent and kissed her lips. Just lightly, just a friendly little kiss, but she felt the shock-wave right down to her toes. 'Goodnight, Ruth. Sleep tight. See you tomorrow.'

'See you tomorrow,' she echoed, wondering vaguely how come they were seeing each other quite so much these days. Not that she was complaining, but—

'Don't come out, it's foul.'

He kissed her again, a peck on the cheek, and she watched him go and wished somehow that he didn't have to leave.

The next two days were a nightmare. The weather was dreadful, lashing rain and strong winds, and she wondered if Mac's parents would get off all right on Tuesday. She was busy at work, visiting all her existing patients and picking up a couple of new ones, too.

One of these was a diabetic who had moved into the area, and he was blind. This meant he had difficulty testing his blood-sugar level to gauge the amount of insulin he needed, and so she was to go every day and test it to make sure he was stable.

She ran up the path to his front door and rang the bell, and seconds later the door opened to reveal a man in his thirties with a lovely retriever by his side. It wasn't in harness, but on the wall behind him Ruth could see a guide dog's harness hanging on the wall.

'You must be Martin Page,' she said. 'How do you do? I'm Ruth Walker, the community nurse.'

He held out his hand and she shook it, pleased to feel a firm, solid handshake. It told her a great deal about a patient, and this man was obviously direct and in command of his life.

'And this must be your guide dog.'

'Yes—Katie. She's off duty—you can talk to her, if you like.'

'Thanks.' She bent forward and offered Katie her hand to sniff. It wouldn't hurt to make friends with her—there might come a time when Martin needed help and she would have to break in with the help of the police. If she and the dog knew each other, it would be less of a problem.

'Come in—let's get out of the wind,' he said, and led her through into an immaculately tidy sitting room. 'I've got my kit here on the table all ready for you,' he told her, indicating a plastic box containing test kits, little strips of finger-prick blades and swabs.

'Right, let's have a look. How do you feel, first of all? Are you well at the moment?'

'Tired,' he confessed. 'Moving is so traumatic. I've had my mother here for a few days, but now she's gone and I've got to find everything on my own. It's a good job I've got a retentive memory.'

'Certainly is. Right, let's have a look at your blood-sugar level while we talk. Any preference for which finger?'

They chatted about where he'd come from while she timed the sample, and then she frowned at the coloured blob on the test strip and compared it to the packet. 'It's a little high—what is it usually?'

'About seven or so.'

'It's nine—perhaps you need to cut back a little on your food, or boost your insulin. When did you last eat?'

'I've just had lunch—that might explain it. I had tinned peaches—I meant to have fish fingers, chips

and beans, but I opened the tin of peaches by accident, so I ate them up as well.'

'Perhaps you were a bit generous with the chips—
and how did you cook them?' she asked, a little
concerned at the thought of him handling spitting,
boiling oil.

'Oven chips,' he said. 'Don't worry, I don't have
a death wish.'

'I'm glad to hear it,' she said with a laugh. 'Well,
it seems reasonably OK. I'll come back tomorrow.
Just keep an eye on what you have today, but don't
cut back drastically.'

'I won't. I don't want a hypo—not when I'm on
my own. It was bad enough when I was married.'

'Are you divorced?' she asked in dismay, wondering how many strikes a man could have against
him.

'I will be soon. She decided it was too much, so
she took the kids and moved out—I couldn't afford
to stay in the house on my own, and my mother
lives near here, so I thought it would be good. I'm
a writer—I don't need to be in town, and here in
the centre of the village I'm near the shop and the
post office. Once I find my way around it should be
fine.'

'People will help you,' she assured him. 'If you
tell them where you live and where you're going,
they'll make sure you don't get lost. Everyone's
very kind—but do be careful crossing the main road.
The traffic can go a bit fast along the top there.'

'I will. Thank you.'

She left him and went on to her next patient, John
Grainger. He seemed to be coping well with his
home-based peritoneal dialysis, and his catheter site

looked clean and healthy. He showed her the latest bag of effluent which he'd saved for her to see. It was clear and as she would have hoped to find it.

'Are you feeling more confident now?' she asked him, and he nodded and smiled.

'Yes, much. I seem to have the right number of hands again.'

'Good. Are you finding your working day pans out, or haven't you started yet?'

His wife snorted. 'Started? I don't think he ever stopped—only by force when he was in hospital. Actually it's worse, because he doesn't get any time to rest. Before he had to go and lie down for a few hours three times a week. Now he doesn't, and he just keeps going. He'll kill himself.'

Ruth laughed and shook her head at him. 'Take it easy. It's still early days. Give yourself time to relax—it's very important.'

'She exaggerates,' he said, and she smiled and left them to it, still arguing about whether he did too much or not.

He was her last call on Monday, and as she hadn't had any messages on her pager, she went straight home to see how the electricians had got on. She found chaos, and the foreman who had hung on to talk to her.

The dogs were huddled in the kitchen looking worried, the cats by and large were out, except for one who'd managed to get back into the airing cupboard and was lurking on the top shelf looking hunted.

She walked round the house, studying each room in turn—the furniture propped up out of the way, the boards up, wires dangling everywhere—and, of course, her existing power was disconnected except in the kitchen and her bedroom, and that, she discovered, would be out the following day.

'And you've got woodworm,' the electrician told her. 'In the roof, and in the little bedroom. It needs treating—the whole house will need treating to be on the safe side, underside of the boards, the joists, the top of the boards, the stairs—all of it. And you can't stay here while that's done, especially not with all the animals. Dead toxic, it is, the stuff they use. Forty-eight hours minimum you have to be out of the place, and you might as well have it done while the boards are up. No point in going through this upheaval twice. I should get a quote, if I were you— maybe they could start Wednesday. I'll be done tomorrow, especially if I don't have to put the boards back down.'

'Right,' she said weakly. 'Fine. Thank you. Cup of tea?'

'No, I won't, my wife'll have my dinner on the table. I'll see you tomorrow, nice and early.'

'Thanks.'

She let him out, went back into the kitchen and stared sightlessly out of the window. More expense—and not just expense, they had to move out! Where on earth were they to go?

There was a knock at the front door and she opened it to find Mac there.

'Hi—are you all right? You look poleaxed.'

'I've got to have woodworm treatment—that means I have to pay another firm to come in and do some essential work, I have to move out into a hotel, I have to put the animals in kennels for a few days— it's going to cost a fortune, and I just don't have it!

And the place is in chaos, and I just want to go and dig Mrs Blewitt up and shout at her! Except I can't,' she added practically, 'because she was cremated.'

Mac laughed. He actually had the darned nerve to laugh at her, and she hit him, a solid fist square in the middle of his chest, and then turned on her heel and stomped into the kitchen.

'Shut the door on your way out,' she yelled, and then felt his firm, warm hands on her shoulders.

'I'm sorry. I just had visions of you frantically digging in the churchyard in a towering paddy in the middle of the night with your nightdress flapping round your ankles, looking like a refugee from a horror movie. It just tickled me.'

'Humph,' she said, slamming mugs down on the worktop. 'I suppose you want a cup of tea now you're here?'

He propped himself up on the worktop and grinned at her. 'I wouldn't mind—if you can promise you won't poison it.'

She rolled her eyes and threw a teabag into each mug, then poured boiling water on them. 'Mac, where the hell am I going to go?' she asked, her anger draining away. 'I can't put them all in kennels—they aren't vaccinated and, anyway, I can't afford it.'

'Can't it come out of her money?'

She chewed her lip. 'Well, I suppose it could, but it doesn't solve the vaccinations, and—oh, I don't know. I just didn't need this—not on top of the wiring and the roof and the windows and the plumbing and everything else!'

'Poor baby,' he said gently, and drew her into his arms. For a moment she gave in to the urge and rested her head on his chest, listening to the steady rhythm of his heart and wallowing in self-pity.

Then she pushed away from him and straightened up. 'Well, I'll just have to do it and somehow find a way to pay for it. I can't let the place be eaten away all around me—I shall lie in bed at night now and listen to them chomping on my boards and worry about the bed falling through the floor!'

Mac chuckled, then, after a second's hesitation, he spoke. 'You could always come and stay with me,' he said quietly. 'God knows there's enough room in the house, and with my parents away from tomorrow you won't be in anyone's way.'

'But what about the animals?' Ruth asked worriedly.

'We've got the old surgery cages out the back—the cats can go in there, and the dogs can just fit in with ours when we're there or be shut in the surgery with their beds during the day. They'll be fine.'

She felt the worry and tension lighten, and suddenly her problems seemed to shrink and fade away. 'OK,' she said. 'If your parents don't mind. You need to ask them, though, it is their house.'

'They won't mind at all. You know that.'

'Please, ask them,' she insisted.

'OK. Then when will you move in? Tomorrow?'

'Will that be all right? I haven't got a timber treatment firm lined up yet.' She glanced at her watch. It was five-fifteen. 'I could try ringing round now,' she said doubtfully.

Mac sipped his tea and watched her over the top of the mug as she made a few phone calls. Finally a local firm agreed to come out that evening and have a look and quote her. 'We're not usually beaten on price, and the only reason we can do it this week is because we've had a cancellation—they've got the flu and can't move out, so you're in luck. I'll see you at seven,' the man promised, and she rang off.

'He's coming at seven—he could do it this week,' she relayed to Mac, and he nodded.

'Fine. I'll tell my parents.'

'Ask them,' she corrected, and he grinned.

'Such a worrywart.' He put his mug down and pulled a syringe in a plastic tube out of his pocket. 'Where's Thomas?'

'On my favourite cushion, I expect. He usually is.'

He was. Mac injected him, patted her cheek and winked at her, and left. Half an hour later he rang to say that his parents were delighted to be able to help, and if there was anything else she needed, just to ask.

Relief made her legs go weak, and when the man came and agreed that they could do the work on Wednesday, and gave her what she felt was a very reasonable quote, she stopped worrying about that and started planning what she and the animals would need until Friday night when they could move back in again.

Ruth spent the evening packing up her clothes that she'd need for the next few days, and the following evening she packed them into the car, together with all the cat and dog food, beds, blankets, bowls and so forth.

Then, when she was all ready to move the animals, she rang Mac and he came round with pet carriers and they loaded the animals into his Discovery and set off.

She felt like Mrs Noah, and wondered if Noah had been the Old Testament equivalent of a vet, or just a softie like Mrs Blewitt.

It took a while to get them all settled, and the cats mewed and fussed and sniffed around in their cages for a while, but the dogs ran around the house, having a wonderful time, and the McWilliams' dogs all but ignored them, so used were they to other animals about the place.

'Well, that was painless,' Mac said with a smile, and picked up her case. 'Come upstairs, I'll show you to your room.'

She followed him up the stairs, turned left at the top and then left again into a pretty bedroom. 'There you go,' he said, putting her case down. 'The bathroom's just next door, and my room's the one beyond it. You shouldn't get lost. I'll see you downstairs—supper's in ten minutes. I'll leave you to unpack.'

It didn't take long. She hung up her tunics for work, and the skirt she'd brought just in case, and put the other things away in the top drawer of the chest by the bed. The bathroom next door was cosy, unlike hers, and she thought longingly of lying in a nice, hot bath and relaxing.

Then she thought of Mac right next door, and suddenly it all seemed a little intimate—just a bit too cosy.

'You're being silly,' she told herself crossly. 'He's just a friend. Deal with it.'

She went downstairs and found him dishing up the supper, a huge casserole that looked suspiciously like something his mother might have made. There were jacket potatoes, lovely and crispy from the Aga, and fresh, lightly cooked broccoli and carrots.

'Smells gorgeous,' she told him. The dogs obviously thought so, too. All of them, his parents' two and her three, were lined up in a row, bottoms down, tails wagging hopefully.

'In your dreams,' Mac said heartlessly, and buried his fork in a chunk of meat. 'Go on, hop it.'

His dogs sighed and lay down. Hers were more optimistic. They wriggled closer, and Toby, who was finding the new regime a bit restrictive on the old digestive system, stood on his hind legs with his paws on her knee and whined.

'Surely you don't feed them at the table?' Mac teased, and she laughed a little self-consciously.

'What, me? Toby, get down, you're giving me away.'

Mac chuckled. 'They can be relied on for that.'

'How did you get on, taking your parents this morning?' she asked, changing the subject rapidly.

'Fine. The wind wasn't so strong near Heathrow. They should be well under way by now. Oh, Dad told me to tell you Lucy Kennedy's all right. They've managed to save her fingers—goodness knows how, but they have. And the horse is looking good.'

'What about the kids in the car?'

He shrugged. 'I don't know about them. I think they were all right. To be honest, I don't really care. They came out of that turning much too fast, trying to cut across in front of me, and they got what they deserved. It was the horse I felt sorry for, and Lucy, of course.'

They finished their meal in a companionable silence, broken only by the odd remark or one of the animals pleading, then finally Mac pushed back his chair. 'Well, boys, aren't you lucky? There's a little bit left.'

The dogs all sprang to attention and trotted after him, and Ruth followed, dishing up the miserable little portions for her three compared to the huge bowlfuls that Mac's big dogs had.

'Looks mean, doesn't it?' she said staring at the little dishes.

'They are somewhat smaller. I eat more than you do, too.'

She laughed wryly. 'Not much. I feel stuffed. I ate far too much.'

'You're not exactly overweight, though,' he said, running his eyes over her in a way that made her feel suddenly aware of every inch of her body—and his. 'You used to be skinny.'

'I used to be a child,' she reminded him.

For a moment he said nothing, then his mouth twisted in a wry smile. 'How time flies,' he said lightly, and turned away. 'Coffee or tea?'

She stared after him, not quite sure what had happened, just knowing something had. Something that was going to make staying here just that little bit more difficult.

Or interesting.

'Coffee, please,' she said, and followed him back to the kitchen.

CHAPTER FIVE

THE next three days were strange. They both seemed to be walking round each other on eggshells, avoiding anything that could remotely be described as an intimate moment, and by Friday Ruth was thoroughly confused.

Had Mac picked up on her awareness of him, and did it embarrass him? Goodness knows, she thought, and gave up worrying about it for a while. She had more than enough to worry about with her patients, her house and her animals, without bringing Mac into the already unstable equation.

Martin Page was getting around the village with his dog Katie, and she passed him a couple of times near the village shop, while he was deep in conversation with one resident or another. He looked happy enough, and when she saw him at home he seemed to be coping all right.

She hoped it would prove to have been the right move for him, after all the upset of his divorce. He'd seen his children last weekend, apparently, and would see them again tomorrow. Apparently they missed the dog, and, having taken on Mrs Blewitt's and seen the result of enforced separation at first hand, Ruth was sure Katie must miss them, too.

Mr Hubbard, of course, had heard that she was staying with Mac and never missed an opportunity to tease her about it.

'Moved in the day his parents caught the plane, I heard,' he'd said the first time he'd mentioned it.

'They knew all about it,' she assured him, wondering why she should have to explain herself to the nosy old boy.

'You still out at the McWilliams' place?' he asked on Friday.

'Yes—till tomorrow. It should be all right to go back to my cottage by then.'

'Wouldn't have done in my day, carrying on like that,' he said, then added, 'Not that things didn't go on, of course. We just didn't admit it, unless we got caught.'

'Nothing is going on,' she told him for the third or fourth time. 'I'm just staying there while my house is sprayed with nasty chemicals.'

'Convenient, though,' he added, having the last word as usual.

She gave up. There was no arguing with him. She was there to collect a blood sample, as he was a little breathless and showing signs of anaemia. She'd tested his urine for blood and had found none, and Dr Carter thought it was probably the result of his poor diet.

She took the blood, refused to rise to the bait again and carried on with her work. She had to pop the blood sample into the surgery at lunchtime, and collect a list of visits to fit in that afternoon. As a result it was after six before she got back to the house, to find that Mac had fed the animals, walked the dogs around the garden and put the supper in the oven.

'Early night on Fridays,' he told her with a smile.

'We finish surgery at four. It's the only civilised
night of the week. How's your house?'

She shook her head. 'Don't know. I haven't been
back. At least after all that wind and rain it's a little
warmer than it has been, so I can have the windows
open and give it all a good blow through. I might
go up there this evening and have a look round.'

'Good idea,' he said. 'I'm going to the pub, so
you'll be on your own. I got collared by a bunch of
old farming boys at lunchtime—I promised to pop
in for a while.'

'How exciting,' she teased.

'I expect it will be. They don't believe in moderation. They all sit around and talk about the crisis
in farming and get pie-eyed. No doubt they'll ply
me with Scotch and I'll have to walk home.'

'Poor baby,' she said unsympathetically, and he
poked his tongue out at her, making her chuckle.

So he was going out. Odd, how she could feel
relieved and disappointed at the same time.

The cottage smelt horrendous. Ruth opened all the
windows and wandered round examining the damage. In truth there was very little, and all the new
sockets and switches looked reassuringly modern. If
it hadn't been for the smell, it would have been fine.

She closed the windows and went back to the
house, but there was no sign of Mac. She stayed up
until eleven, then gave up and shut her dogs away,
cuddled the cats and promised them their freedom
the next morning, and went upstairs to bed.

She didn't hear him come in, but something woke
her at two. She lay awake and listened for an age,
then looked out of the window. His car was back,

but only the hall light spilled out across the drive. Had he just come in? Surely he would have come up?

Ruth needed a drink. She hesitated for a moment, but thirst made her get up and pull on her dressing-gown, then cautiously open her door. There was no sound, and she crept downstairs and went into the kitchen on bare, silent feet.

He was in the kitchen, sitting at the table in the dark, staring into a mug. He looked up when she went in, his eyes strangely dark in the dim light from the hall.

'Hi,' he said softly. 'Did I wake you? I came down for a drink.'

'Snap,' she said with a smile. 'How were the farmers?'

'Much as I'd expected. I got away with two whiskies, so I thought I'd risk the short drive home. Do you want tea?'

'Thanks.' She moved past him to get a mug, just as he stood up, and he bumped into her.

'Sorry.' His hands came up to steady her just as she turned, and his hand brushed her breast. For a seemingly endless moment they stood there, frozen, then he lifted his hand and cupped her chin, turning her to face him and staring searchingly into her eyes.

'Ruth?' he murmured.

She lifted her face as his head came down, and their lips brushed, just lightly, just enough to send fire skittering through her veins and put her heart in jeopardy.

'Mac?' she breathed.

His head came down again, and his arms slid round her, lifting her against his chest and crushing her to him as his mouth plundered hers. His tongue sought hers, tangling with it, slowly withdrawing and teasing, then thrusting again as his body rocked against her, hard and urgent.

There were no words. There was nothing to say. They both knew what was happening, and neither of them seemed to know how to stop it. His chest heaved under her hands, and beneath her palm she could feel the solid thud of his heart slamming against his ribs.

His hands fumbled the belt of her dressing-gown, then drew the sides apart, sliding his hands up under her nightshirt to cup the soft fullness of her breasts. A deep, shuddering groan echoed in the darkness, and he pushed the nightshirt up higher and bent his head, taking one taut, aching nipple into his mouth.

She cried out, her hands pulling aside his dressing-gown, and with a groan he eased closer, pressing himself up against her.

She cried out again, all her breath dragged from her lungs by the sensation of his body so close to hers. So close, and yet still too far away.

He lifted her easily, laying her back on the table and locking her legs around his waist, then with a single thrust he entered her, burying himself deep inside her with a ragged cry.

The sensation shattered her. Nothing had ever felt so good, so right, so much. He moved, thrusting again and again into her, driving her higher. She clawed at him, begging him for more, and then suddenly the climax hit her, catapulting her into ecstasy.

He convulsed against her, crying out her name in a broken gasp, and then he held her, his arms locked

around her as the sensation ebbed away, leaving her
stunned.

She felt hot tears sting her eyes, and blinked them
away.

'Mac?' she said, bewildered, and with a muttered
curse he withdrew from her and dragged his dressing-gown closed, belting it tightly around his waist.

He looked as confused as she felt. Oh, God, she
thought, what have we done? She sat up, pulling her
nightshirt down and sliding off the edge of the table,
suddenly terribly embarrassed and shy. What had
she been thinking about? What had *they* been thinking about?

He ran his hands through his hair, and she could
see they were trembling. His chest was still rising
and falling raggedly, and he met her eyes and looked
hastily away.

'I'm sorry,' he rasped. 'God, Ruth, I'm sorry. I
don't know where the hell that came from.'

'Nor do I,' she said unsteadily. She sat down on
a chair, too shocked to stand any longer, unable to
walk away. 'I thought you were upstairs. I didn't
come down looking for you, I swear—'

'Ruth, don't. It isn't your fault. If it's anyone's,
it's mine.'

He sounded agonised, and she reached out and
touched him. He jerked, then turned and met her
eyes, and she saw confusion and sorrow etched on
his face. He shook his head slowly as if in disbelief.

'God, Ruth, I'm sorry. I never meant— If this
wrecks our relationship I'll never forgive myself.
You mean so much to me. You've been such a good
friend over the years, and if I've ruined that I shall
just be gutted.'

He turned away, ramming trembling hands through his hair again, and without thinking she stood up and put her arms round him. 'Mac, it's all right,' she promised him. 'Really. You mean the world to me, too. That hasn't changed.'

He slid his arms round her and hugged her hard against his chest, and she felt the tears well in her eyes and spill down over her cheeks.

Ruth was crying. Damn, she was crying, and he wanted to cry, too, because he'd taken something good and decent and honest and—

What? What had he done to it? Granted, it had been sudden and violent and a little wild, but he didn't regret a second of it, not really. How could he? It had been better than he could ever have imagined it would be, and God knows they'd both been ready for it.

But like that, without warning, on his mother's kitchen table...

Mac groaned and hugged her closer, rocking her and shushing her as she cried, and in his mind's eye he pictured them all sitting round the table just a few days ago, having supper. He'd made biscuits on that table with his mother when he was three years old, for goodness' sake!

He clamped down on the hysterical sob that was rising in his chest and smoothed a soothing hand over her hair. 'It's all right, sweetheart,' he murmured, and hoped to God he was right.

'I'm sorry, I don't know why I'm crying,' she said damply, and sniffed and pushed away from him, grabbing a sheet of kitchen roll and blowing her nose.

'Better?' he said gently, and she nodded.

'Why don't we have that drink you came down for and talk about this?' he went on, and she nodded again and sat down on the nearest chair, staring up at him blankly.

'What happened, Mac?' she asked in bewilderment. 'One minute we were friends, the next— wham! We're there, on the table…' She trailed off, dragging a hand through her tangled hair, pulling it back off her face so he could see the mark on her neck where he'd bitten her.

Heat rose in him again, sudden and urgent and utterly unexpected, and he slammed the kettle on the hob and stood hunched over it, hands on the front rail of the Aga, eyes shut tight to block out the images. He could still see her, though, still feel her writhing under him—

'Mac? The kettle's boiling.'

He pulled two mugs out of the cupboard, threw teabags into them and then mashed them viciously with the spoon.

'Not too strong for me,' she said a little hesitantly, and he fished the teabags out and gave her the one that had the intact teabag. The milk was on the worktop, and he put it on the table and sat down quickly before she realised that his body was betraying him.

'So—what happens now?' she asked, her voice still slightly unsteady with shock.

'I don't know. What do you want to happen now?' he asked gently.

She gave a tiny shrug, a small and strangely helpless gesture that tore at his heart. The desire left him, driven out by that tiny shift of her shoulders that spoke such volumes, and he cursed himself mentally for hurting her—Ruth, always so sweet, so funny, so straightforward and brave and honest.

His Ruth now. Oh, God.

'Can we start again?' she said quietly. 'I mean, I know we can't turn the clock back and go back to how we were, but can we start again from when we met this time? I don't know why this happened, but I've been feeling more and more aware of you ever since we met again—but I thought it was just one-sided. I never dreamt you felt like that—if you did. I don't know, maybe you don't. Maybe it was just a knee-jerk reaction to an available woman—'

'No,' he said firmly, cutting her off before she went on and damned him any more. 'No, Ruth, it was more than that. I've been feeling the same, and I thought it was just me. Then, just now I realised it wasn't, and…' He shrugged. 'I don't know what happened either, Ruth. I just hope I don't live to regret it, because it was beautiful.'

He swallowed. His voice was rough with desire, but he couldn't do anything about it, and, dammit, she might as well know that he found her attractive.

'I know it wasn't romantic or seductive or any of the other things that women like, but at least it was honest, Ruth, and although I might live to regret what it does to us, I'll never regret that something so beautiful happened between us.'

Her eyes filled with tears, and she looked down into her tea, her hair falling forward and making a screen around her face, hiding her expression.

Mac wanted to reach forward and lift the hair away so he could see her face, but he didn't. He gave her her privacy. He didn't know her well enough to pry. Not now, not in this context. He felt suddenly very unsure, something that was foreign to him. How did he handle this relationship now? Go back to the beginning, she'd said. Start again.

'Ruth?'

She lifted her head, and he could see the twin tracks of her tears down her cheeks. 'Yes?' she said softly, and in her eyes he could see forgiveness and something else. Something that might have been the first tiny sparks of what might grow to be love.

'Let's start again,' he suggested 'From tomorrow. Let's see where it takes us—see how we both feel. To be honest, I have very little idea how I do feel. It was so sudden, so unexpected—it's like being in uncharted territory. We ought to give it a try—who knows where we might end up?'

Her smile touched his heart. 'Who knows?' She stood up and put her mug in the sink. 'Mac—do you mind if we don't sleep together?' she asked hesitantly. 'I just feel—I need some space. Time to think.'

'Sure,' he agreed.

'I know it's locking the stable door after the horse has bolted,' she went on, 'but I really mean it about going back to square one. One minute we were friends, the next we were lovers. There should be something in between. I don't know this side of you, I've never seen it. I need to—I need time to get to know you—Andrew McWilliam, the man, not Mac, the boy I grew up with. And you need to know me.'

He nodded. She was right, he didn't really know her any more. He'd made a whole load of assumptions, but they might well be wrong.

'Sure,' he said, and then, before she left the room,

he added, 'Talking of shutting the stable door after
the horse has bolted, I don't suppose there's the re-
motest chance that you're on the Pill?'

She spun to face him, her eyes wide with shock.
'Oh, my God! I never even thought...' She shook
her head. 'No. I'm not on the Pill—why would I be?
I don't do this sort of thing!' She broke off on a
slightly hysterical little laugh, and shook her head
again.

'I'll see the doctor in the morning. He's in the
surgery. I'll ask him for a prescription for the morning-after pill. It works very well if you take it
quickly.'

'Ruth—' He broke off, hardly daring to say the
words, then went on, 'Ruth, if it doesn't work—
don't have an abortion, will you? Please? Or, at
least, tell me if you're pregnant and talk about it
first.'

Her face softened. 'It will work—and if it didn't,
there's no way I'd hurt your baby, Andrew.'

Andrew, he thought. Not Mac any more. Not
now. He swallowed a huge lump in his throat and
watched her go, then dropped his head in his hands
and sighed.

One minute they were friends, the next they were
talking about being parents!

She was right. Nothing would ever be the same
again...

Amazingly, Ruth slept well, and then first thing in
the morning she packed up her things and ferried
her animals back to her cottage. There had been a
note from Mac on the kitchen table—the table where

it had all happened. She'd stroked her fingers thoughtfully over the old wood and closed her eyes.

She'd told herself she had to stop remembering it, reliving it. It had just been a moment of madness, just one of those stupid things that people sometimes did. It had probably meant nothing. Men did things like that—her father had all the time, or so she'd understood as she'd grown older. What if he was like her father? She didn't know anything about Mac any more, really, except that he was on the rebound from a very messy affair that had damaged his pride.

What if she'd just been a way to bolster his ego? After all, he hadn't even stuck around to talk this morning. Oh, God, please, no, she'd thought with a wave of dread so powerful it had frightened her. Let it be real. He hadn't walked out, anyway. He'd left the note, saying he'd gone to the practice for morning surgery and would ring her later.

Not that she gave him much chance to ring. She was out for most of the morning, first at the surgery asking Tom Carter for a prescription for the morning-after pill and dealing with his gentle teasing and I-told-you-sos, then at the chemist getting the pills and taking the first dose, then in the electricity showroom ordering four efficient modern storage heaters for her house.

Then she went home to find a message on her answerphone, and a note through her door.

Mac, worrying about her.

No, not Mac. Andrew.

She swallowed the emotion that still threatened to overwhelm her, and rang him at home.

'I wondered if you were all right—I thought perhaps the fumes—'

'Idiot,' she teased gently. 'I'm fine. I had to go shopping.'

'Shopping?' he asked in disbelief.

'Yes—for storage heaters. Oh, and I got the prescription,' she added warily.

'Oh. Right. Good.'

Was she imagining it, or did he sound disappointed? No, she was imagining it. There was no way—was there?

'I didn't mean to run away like that and worry you, but I wanted to get the animals settled again, so I thought it would make sense. Anyway, you were busy, but I didn't want you to think I'd run out without thanking you for having me.'

There was a second's stunned silence, then he gave a strangled laugh. 'I take you didn't mean that the way I heard it,' he said softly, and she felt herself colour to the roots of her hair.

'No,' she confirmed wryly. 'I meant thank you for having us all to stay—for putting us up. It was very good of you.'

'Don't,' he said, his voice gruff. 'Don't thank me, Ruth—not after what happened. I behaved with all the finesse of a randy teenager.'

'You weren't alone,' she reminded him softly.

'No. No, I suppose I wasn't. Are you busy tonight?'

She felt instantly wary. 'Why?'

'I thought I could bring round a take-away or something, and we could start this getting-to-know-each-other thing—but if you're busy, that's OK.'

'I'm not busy,' she said truthfully. 'That would be nice—only eat first. I'm not very hungry. Those pills make you feel a bit grim.'

She could feel the guilt coming off him in waves, and almost smiled. Almost. She felt too queasy to really enjoy the humour in the situation.

'I'll see you at seven,' he said, and rang off.

By seven Ruth really did feel grim, and she was very glad she'd asked Mac to eat first. He arrived on time and came in when she called out. He found her in the sitting room, curled up on her chair with a cat on her lap, probably looking like death warmed up. She'd scraped her hair up into a clip at the back of her head, and it felt tight and she wished she hadn't done it, because she couldn't put her head back and close her eyes, which was what she really wanted to do.

He looked gorgeous. Good enough to eat, if she'd had any appetite, which she didn't—not even for him.

He took one look at her and sighed harshly. 'You look awful,' he said bluntly. 'Ruth, I'm so sorry—'

'Stop apologising,' she told him. 'Put the kettle on, I need a cup of weak tea. I'll let you wait on me.'

He pulled his hand out from behind his back and handed her a bunch of freesias. They smelt wonderful—strong enough to drown out the chemical from the timber treatment—and they brought tears to her eyes.

'Thank you,' she said unevenly, and looked up in time to see the pleasure on his face.

He gave a wry smile, and didn't seem to know what to do with his hands. 'I'll—er—put the kettle on, then,' he said, and shot into the kitchen.

She smiled to herself. He seemed so uneasy—like

an awkward adolescent on his best behaviour. Poor Mac.

She got to her feet and followed him out, plonking the flowers in the sink for the moment, then she went up on tiptoe and kissed him.

He groaned and drew her gently, cautiously, into his arms, and kissed her back. 'I've been wanting to do that for hours,' he admitted, lifting his head after a moment. 'Nothing wild, nothing too much, just a kiss. And a hug. I've really needed a hug.'

'Me, too,' she confessed, and went back into his arms.

Maybe it would be all right, she thought. Maybe they hadn't lost anything. Maybe they'd gained— and if not, she would still have that one amazing, wonderful experience to remember…

Martin Page looked worried when she arrived at his house on Monday morning. 'Everything all right?' she asked, concerned.

'It's Katie—she seems a bit off colour. I don't know what's wrong with her. The children were here over the weekend, and I don't know if they gave her anything to eat, but she's still quite young and I try and be careful not to leave things lying around that she might chew. Anyway, she's been sick a couple of times, and I know the vet's a friend of yours—you couldn't give him a ring for me, could you, and ask him if he could take a look at her?'

'Sure. I'll call him.'

He was right, she thought, looking at the dog. She did look ill. She left a message at the surgery, and Mac rang her in her lunch-hour.

'I've got Martin Page's dog in—she's got an obstruction in her intestine, and I'm going to have to operate. He'll be without her for a few days, so I thought you ought to know.'

'Poor thing. She's a lovely dog. Will she be all right?'

'Yes, I hope so. I haven't operated on her yet, but I thought I might pop in and talk to him later about her—want to come with me?'

'Sure. What time?'

'Seven? I thought we might go out for a quick bite in the pub, if you like, afterwards.'

'What's the matter,' she teased, 'run out of your mother's cooking?'

He chuckled. 'Almost. I just thought it might be nice. It's quiet on a Monday.'

'OK,' she agreed, and he picked her up at seven with the news that Katie had had a lump of rubber stuck in her pyloric sphincter. 'It looks like a bit of a dog toy,' he said, 'so perhaps while we're there we should check that the rest of her toys are all right.'

Martin Page was relieved to hear that his faithful and much-loved dog was recovering, and he was puzzled about the dog toy. 'Yes, she does have one,' he said. 'I don't know where it is—it's blue.'

'Here,' Mac said, pulling a mangled toy out from under the table in the corner. 'I suspect the children being here might have made her a bit edgy and over-excited. Sometimes under those circumstances they can take it out on their toys. I should throw it out, if I were you, then it won't happen again.'

'And when will she be back?' he asked worriedly. 'I mean, to recover, not to work.'

'Tomorrow, if you can manage? And she should be able to work again a little in a couple of days—just the odd stroll to the shop and so on. I wouldn't go for a long walk, but it's amazing how quickly dogs recover, and a little activity will be good for her. And she'll need very light food—nothing but liquid for a couple of days. OK?'

He chatted for a few more minutes about her treatment and the operation, and then they left him and went to the pub.

'Poor guy,' Mac said sympathetically. 'Fancy being diabetic and blind.'

'And divorced,' Ruth added. 'Makes you realise how lucky we are, doesn't it?'

He looked down at her thoughtfully.

'It certainly does,' he said, and dropped a swift, gentle kiss on her lips. 'Come on, let's go and eat. I'm starving.'

CHAPTER SIX

ON WEDNESDAY Ruth discovered that she wasn't pregnant. Odd, that funny little wave of disappointment. She didn't get time to think about it, though, because it was one of those days.

She went to see Martin Page and saw him through the window collapsed on the floor of the sitting room, Katie standing worriedly beside him and whining.

She called the police, and they came instantly and opened the door with a set of skeleton keys. Katie greeted her with what looked suspiciously like relief, and Ruth went straight to Martin's side and checked the pulse in his neck.

To her relief she found it, but it was a good job the police had been quick, she thought, because he seemed to be in a deep hypoglycaemic coma. 'It's all right, Katie,' she said reassuringly. 'Good girl.'

'Is he alive?' the policeman asked worriedly.

'Yes.' She finger-pricked Martin and squeezed a drop of blood onto a test strip. 'Yes—he's in a hypo. He must have had too much insulin by accident, or not eaten his breakfast in time.' His blood sugar was dangerously low, below one, and she quickly gave him a glucagon injection and waited for him to come round.

'Martin?' she said, shaking him gently. 'Martin, wake up. Come on, now, time for breakfast.'

He groaned and rolled over, and she rolled him

back and shook him again, pushing him into wake-fulness.

'Head aches,' he mumbled, closing his eyes again, and she propped him up and forced him to drink a carton of milkshake from his fridge, kept especially for the purpose.

'Disgusting,' he said, pushing it away. 'I'm going to be sick.'

True to his word, he retched half-heartedly, and she mopped him up and stuck the straw back in his mouth.

'Come on, Martin, please,' she cajoled. 'Have another sip—that's good. And another.'

'Will you be all right now, Nurse?' one of the policeman said, hovering in the background. She glanced over her shoulder and saw him edging towards the door, looking distinctly green. There was no sign of the other one—he must have already gone. Funny how so many people couldn't cope with sickness.

'We'll be fine. Thank you very much. You've been a great help.'

'Glad to be of service, love,' he said, and disappeared.

'I really don't want this,' Martin moaned, pushing the carton aside.

'You have to have it, Martin, and I can't leave you until you've had a proper breakfast and your blood sugar's looking normal again. High would be good. Can you think why this happened?'

'Missed my breakfast—Katie was sick, and I had to clear it up. It's difficult when you can't see, and I didn't want to risk treading in it. I suppose it just took longer than I thought.'

Looking round, Ruth could see a few marks on the carpet, and while he sipped the rest of the drink under protest, she cleaned up the mess the dog had made and then checked Katie to see if she was all right.

The dog's incision looked a little angry, so she rang Mac and he nipped out of surgery to see her. Katie obligingly lay down and rolled over, and he peered at her tummy and winced.

'Ouch, yes, it does look a little sore. It needs bathing with saline—I don't suppose you'd like to do that as part of your routine, would you?' Mac grinned at Ruth with that little-boy charm, and she sighed.

'Like I have nothing else to do all day,' she grumbled goodnaturedly, and then relented. 'OK, OK, I'll do it. What about antibiotics?'

'I'm putting them in her food,' Martin told them. 'Or I was. I don't know why she was sick.'

'Just upset after the anaesthetic, I expect. I'll give her a couple of injections now to settle her down and knock that infection on the head, and then she should start to improve almost immediately. Keep an eye on her, Ruth, could you, and if this redness doesn't settle, can you let me know?'

'Of course. Poor Katie,' she crooned, stroking her gently, and then she looked across at Martin. 'Have you finished that drink yet?'

'Bully,' he murmured. 'Not quite, I don't think. It's still sloshing.'

'Drink up, then.'

He gave a hollow laugh. 'Have you ever drunk anything like this when you're feeling sick? Trust me, it's foul.'

'I know,' she said with sympathy. 'I'm sorry. I hate having to bully you, but it has to be done. How's your headache?'

'Awful.'

Mac finished injecting the dog and got to his feet. 'I'll see you out,' Ruth said, and followed him to the door, pausing to look up at him and taking a second just to enjoy the view. She felt better just looking at him.

'Thanks for coming over,' she murmured. 'It was that or put her in my car and bring her to you, and, with her chucking up, I wasn't too sure I wanted to do that!'

'I can understand that,' he said with a chuckle, then searched her eyes. It was strange how blue his eyes looked in some lights, she thought dreamily. 'Are you busy tonight?' he asked. 'I thought we could go out for a drink.'

Even the thought of the noisy pub made her tired. 'No, not busy, but I wouldn't mind an evening in. Want to watch TV?' she suggested.

'Could do. I have to do the stock at home after I finish work—I won't get away until nearly eight tonight, I don't think. Is that too late?'

She shook her head. 'That's fine. Shall I feed you?'

He smiled. 'Will I be safe?'

'Probably.'

'Yes, then. Thanks.' He winked, and, bending forward, dropped a swift kiss on her lips. 'See you at eight.'

She closed the door and went back to Martin, to find him starting to drift out again. 'Martin, come on,' she said, and resorted to bullying and cajoling to get him to finish the drink. Then she made him eat cereal with sugar and lots of milk, and then finally she left him to rest, with a promise to see him later.

'Thanks,' he said sincerely, as she was leaving. 'I do appreciate what you've done. That's the only thing that worries me about living alone—going into a hypo and not being able to get help.'

'But you don't,' Ruth said slowly. 'You have Katie. How about training her to bark when you pass out? She never barks normally. Maybe the guide dogs association could do something?'

'It's a thought,' he said slowly. 'I'll give them a ring.'

She left him planning, and had to rush round her other patients. She checked him again before she finished for the day, and found him much better and with a blood-sugar level that was much more acceptable. Katie, too, seemed a little better, and was pleased to see her, as usual. Ruth bathed the dog's incision, although she didn't really have time, and the dog lay patiently and seemed almost grateful.

'How about a cup of tea?' Martin suggested when she'd finished, but she declined.

'I have to get back—I've got my animals to see to,' she told him. 'Perhaps another time.'

He looked so crestfallen she felt guilty, but she was already behind and had a lot to do before Mac came over. And, of course, when she got in her animals were clamouring for food. 'I know, I know, I'm late,' she said, not even bothering to stop and take her coat off. She did a quick head count, found they were all present and correct and put the kettle on.

Cup of tea, light the fire and get cleaned up, then supper, she thought, but remembered with dismay that her fridge was all but empty and she'd been meaning to go shopping tonight.

Oh, well, she'd have to be creative and do something clever with pasta!

'That was lovely,' Mac said, pushing his plate away and smiling at her.

'You're too kind,' she said with a laugh. 'It was a real pot luck. If I hadn't had the jar of spaghetti sauce, we would have starved!'

'It was out of a jar?' he said with wide-eyed innocence, but she caught sight of the twinkle and threw the wet dishcloth at him.

'Just for that, you can wash up,' she scolded, and then belatedly remembered that meant her standing beside him drying up—hip to hip.

Still, it had been said now, and she supposed if they were going to get to know 'that side' of each other, they'd have to put themselves in situations where they were aware of each other. Her heart seemed to crawl up her throat and started banging away above her collar-bones, surely visible. She was aware enough of him already!

'Come on, then, lazybones,' he was saying, clearing the table with speed. 'Where's the washing-up liquid? Come along, jump to it. I don't want to be doing this all night.'

'Let's leave it,' Ruth said, clutching at straws, but he wasn't having any of it, and moments later she was next to him, wiping up glasses and plates and cutlery and pots, and trying not to lean forward as he reached over so that her breast brushed his arm yet again...

'Are you doing that on purpose?' Mac asked with a glint of humour in his eyes.

'In your dreams,' she replied in her best put-down voice, but it didn't seem to work.

He dropped the dishcloth, took the teatowel out of her hands and looped it over her head, and drew her inexorably closer. 'You are a tease,' he murmured, just before his lips came down and covered hers.

'I'm not,' she protested against his lips. 'It was an accident!'

'And pigs fly,' he added, drawing her closer. 'Kiss me again and tell me that.'

She pushed away from him, and to her disappointment he let her go. Not far, though. He stood on her side of the little sink, nudging up against her whenever he thought he could get away with it, which was pretty much all the time, and when the last item had been dried and put away, he drew her into his arms, nuzzled her neck gently and sighed.

'I want to make love to you,' he said quietly. 'I know I can't. I'm just telling you—part of our policy of being honest.'

Had that really been her idea? It was absolutely the last thing she needed to know tonight! She felt heat searing through her, leaving her weak and helpless. 'Damn you,' she said with affection. 'I wish you hadn't said that—and anyway, we can't. I'm—what was it they used to say? Indisposed? I'm not pregnant.'

He went still, then hugged her gently. 'Are you feeling OK?'

'Bit rough. That's why I didn't want to go out.'

He hugged her again. 'Oh, well. Since wild sex is off the menu, how about lighting the fire and settling down to a bit of television instead?' he said with a grin.

She smiled back. 'Good idea. The fire's lit,' she told him. 'Go and sit down and I'll bring us drinks. Coffee?'

'Thanks. I'll go and start clearing cats out of the way.'

He went into the sitting room, and while she made the coffee she listened to him—the hardened professional vet, the tough guy who had to make the *hard decisions*—cuddling and oochy-coochying the cats and dogs in a daft voice without a trace of self-consiousness.

The coffee made, she followed him through and paused in the doorway, smiling indulgently at him as he snuggled the vicious and unlovely Thomas in his arms and crooned to him.

'He seems to be doing really well,' he said with a smile. 'I think he's forgiven me—'

Mac had spoken too soon. A razor-tipped paw whipped out and zapped his face, and with a howl of indignation Mac dropped the cat and clapped a hand over his cheek.

'Perhaps not,' Ruth said with a stifled smile.

'Ouch, damn, that hurt!' he protested, looking round for the cat, a cushion poised to hurl at the vindictive beast.

'Let me look,' she said, peeling away his fingers one by one and inspecting the slash. 'It's a good 'un,' she said, and he glared at her.

'You don't have to sound so pleased—or so proud of the damn cat!'

Ruth worked a little harder on stifling the smile. 'Just passing comment,' she corrected.

'Don't bother,' he growled, and winced again as she dabbed at the scratch with a swab. 'Be careful, woman, that hurts!'

'You are such a baby,' she told him disgustedly, slopping antiseptic freely in the wound. His lips slapped shut, his mouth firmed to a grim line and he said nothing.

He didn't speak again until it was all cleaned up and she'd rubbed antiseptic cream into the area. Then he shot her a malevolent glare. 'You don't have to enjoy it so much,' he grumbled.

'Sorry, I didn't quite hear that.'

'Thank you,' he said ungraciously. 'Ouch, that stings. Is he always so changeable?'

She shook her head. 'Oh, no. Usually he doesn't even bother to purr at other people before he goes for them. Trust me, you're not the first. I'm just amazed you've got away with it for so long!'

He took the coffee off the mantelpiece and settled down in one of the chairs after clearing it yet again of interlopers. 'How's Toby? He's looking thinner,' he said, changing the subject and subjecting the innocent little dog to a jaundiced glare.

'He is thinner. It's dropping off him now he can't sneak off to my next-door neighbours to steal their catfood. It's brilliant, and he's more playful and he's got more energy.' She paused, feeling a pang of guilt. 'Mac, I'm sorry about your face.'

His eyes locked with hers, and gradually the steely expression faded and a slow, reluctant smile bathed his features. 'It's OK,' he murmured. 'It happens all the time. I just hate it. I feel as if they've won some imaginary war game if they manage to land a swipe—I'm usually quicker than that. You must have distracted me.'

She laughed. 'That's right, blame it on me.'

'Well, it has to be someone's fault,' he teased gently. 'Oh, by the way,' he went on, 'talking of someone's fault, I bumped into Mike Foster earlier today—I gave him some advice last week and wouldn't charge him, so for my sins he gave me two tickets to the Young Farmers' Christmas Ball on Saturday. Fancy going?'

The Young Farmers' Ball. Heavens. She hadn't been for years—not since they'd all gone together in a group when she'd been seventeen—the last year before everyone had started to go away to university and the group had dispersed for good.

'Who's the band?' she asked, pretending an academic interest when all she could think about was that she would dance with him, and feel his arms around her, and sway with his body to the music.

'Not sure what they're called—does it matter?'

She shook her head, avoiding his eye. 'No, it doesn't matter at all. Are you sure you've got time to go?'

He laughed. 'Probably not. I'm working on Saturday morning at the surgery but I'm not on call, at least. I'll have to do the stock early that evening and again in the morning on Sunday—so no lazy lie-in, but that's what you get for growing older, I suppose. What about you? When are you on duty?'

She wrinkled her nose. 'Saturday and Sunday. There seem to be plenty of us at the moment, so we're working one weekend on, one off, then sharing a weekend. It's my turn for the weekend on, but we don't do evenings or nights, just eight to five like civilised people—'

'Who are you calling uncivilised?' he asked with a grin, stretching and filling the entire space in front of the fire with his long, rangy body. The little sitting room was too small—far too small for so much taut, sexy male on display!

She kicked his ankle. 'Make yourself at home,' she said drily, and he chuckled and pulled his leg out of reach.

'So, will you come with me,' he teased, 'or do I have to go into the pub and pull some nubile young bit of totty?'

'If you could find one to have you,' she retorted, a little shocked by the sudden surge of jealousy at the thought of him with another woman—especially a *nubile young bit of totty*, for heaven's sake! 'Yes, I'll come,' she added hastily, before he could take her up on her rather foolish challenge.

There wasn't the slightest doubt that if he walked into the pub and said, 'Who wants to come with me to the ball?' he'd have a rush of applicants from eight to eighty—and Mrs Frayne would no doubt send a postal application!

He didn't seem about to try it, anyway. Instead he allowed Fluff, the big ginger queen, to jump up on his lap and snuggle down for a cuddle. The dogs were all flat out in front of the fire, and the only sound in the room was the odd crackle from the fire, the purring of the cats and the tick of the old grandfather clock on the wall behind her.

They were supposed to be watching the television, she remembered, but it was peaceful without it, and Mac seemed happy enough. She rested her head back against the wing of the chair, closed her eyes and let herself drift off.

Mac woke her much later, when the fire had died right down and the moon was high, and she went with him to the door and kissed him goodnight, a long, slow, lazy kiss that made her want to ask him to stay—not to make love, but just to hold her, to be there for her.

She wanted it so much it almost scared her. She watched him go, put the dogs out, locked up and went alone to her bed, huddling under the chilly covers and thinking about him, and why she wanted him so badly.

There was only one answer, and she wasn't ready for it. It was too soon, she didn't know him. Not like that, as a lover. As a friend, yes, but not as a partner in life's trials—someone to share the ups and downs of her day, to help with the little things that needed more than two hands, to hold her in the still hours of the night...

The yearning ache almost took her breath away.

She wasn't going to see so much of Mac, she decided as she drove along a deserted lane the next morning. That wild moment of weakness on his mother's kitchen table had been just that, she told herself—a wild moment of weakness. They shouldn't let it force them into a relationship they weren't ready for. He'd only just split up with Krista, she reminded herself. He didn't need another demanding relationship, and she wasn't built for anything else.

There was no way she could indulge in an on-off affair like the one they'd had. She'd want it all.

Damn it, she *did* want it all—and he wasn't made that way. He didn't want to settle down or else he would have done. There was no way there'd been a shortage of opportunity, either at vet school or since. All those pretty little female vets, the veterinary nurses, the clients—heavens, there was no end of opportunity.

Not like her job, where she spent her life visiting the elderly or terminally ill.

No, she decided, she'd see less of him. She wouldn't let them have cosy nights by the fire, like last night. Too dangerous for her heart. She didn't need to have it broken.

She pulled over at the side of the road and studied the address again. Little Ash Lodge. Big house, opposite a junction, the directions said. She turned round and drove back slowly, but the only house she could see opposite a junction was derelict. There couldn't be anyone living there—the roof was falling in and the house was in imminent danger of collapse.

She pulled over and studied it. One of the doors was hanging slightly ajar, despite the cold, and there were no lights on inside. Was it possible her patient lived here? She'd discharged herself from hospital before they could set up a care plan, apparently, and the hospital liaison nurse had asked her to call and check that everything was all right and to monitor her.

There was a crudely painted notice on the front gate that said BEWARE DOGS in runny red letters. She opened the gate warily, and was greeted by a chorus of barking. Two scrawny, mangy dogs hurled themselves out of the door and stood firm in front of her, baying furiously. They were desperately underweight, their eyes wild, and she felt hopelessly out of her depth.

Now what? she thought. Do I challenge them? What do I do? Where's Mac when I need him?

Don't look them in the eye, she remembered. Just stand sideways and hold out your hand, and let them smell you.

She did, and they approached cautiously and sniffed her, then backed off again. Well, at least they hadn't bitten her—yet.

'Mrs Rudge?' she called. 'Are you there?'

She heard a feeble noise, a sort of whimper, and the dogs whined and ran back inside, then came out again. One of them was limping badly, she noticed. 'Can I come in, boys?' she asked them, and moved towards the door. 'Mrs Rudge?'

Even before she reached the door she could smell the room. Mrs Rudge had clearly been incontinent for some time, and as Ruth moved inside and her eyes adjusted to the light, she had to bite back a gasp of horror at the squalid conditions under which the woman was living.

Everything seemed to happen in the one room. There was a kettle and a cooker, both filthy and caked with grease, the floor was littered thickly with stinking, soggy newspapers, and in the bed in the corner lay a feeble, frail old woman with the oldest face Ruth had ever seen.

'Hello, there,' she said gently, and went and crouched beside her bed, taking her hand. The dogs stood guard warily, and she forced herself to ignore

them. 'I'm Ruth, the community nurse,' she told
Mrs Rudge. 'I've come to see how you are—I gather
you discharged yourself from hospital?'

'Had to,' she said weakly. 'My animals—had to
feed them.'

'Wasn't there anyone else who could do it?'

'Too many—but I can't. Too weak. Can't get
up...'

Heavy tears rolled down her cheeks, and Ruth
patted her hand and stood up. 'Don't worry. I'm
going to put the kettle on to make you a hot drink,
and then I'll feed them for you. Is it just the dogs?'

She shook her head. 'Cats—outside. Lots. Feed
in the bin. And the pony—at the back. Needs hay
and water...'

She trailed off and her head dropped back on the
filthy pillow. She was clearly exhausted, and should
have still been in hospital. She'd been admitted with
acute pneumonia and, judging by her pallor, it was
rapidly growing worse.

Ruth was torn. There was no way she could clean
the woman up, not in these conditions. There was
no bedding, she didn't suppose, other than what was
on the bed, and Mrs Rudge was so agitated about
her animals that she was exhausting herself.

'I'll go and see to them now,' Ruth promised, and
put the kettle on, then went outside into the fresh
air. It tasted so sweet and clean she almost over-
dosed on it before she went round the back of the
house to look for the animals.

As she went into the enclosed yard, cats appeared,
running towards her on spindly legs, mewing pa-
thetically and pleading for food. They were thin to

the point of emaciation, their coats scruffy, their eyes dull. Poor, wormy little things, she thought.

She found the feed bin and put out a few scoops onto the ground in a barn, and put some fresh water down in a big enamel bowl. Then she put her head over the gate at the back and drew in a sharp breath.

The pony looked horrendous. He could hardly stand, and his spine and hips and ribs stuck out so much he looked like a skeleton. 'Poor boy,' she murmured, and clambered over the gate to go and have a closer look at him.

Her first step into the muddy enclosure took her in over her ankle, and she stopped. She had to deal with Mrs Rudge, and there was nothing she could do for the pony anyway. She turned back, pulling her foot out of the mud with a squelch, and wiped it on the grass outside before taking out her mobile phone and ringing Tom Carter.

'She'll have to go back in,' Ruth told him softly, 'but I don't want to be the one to tell her. She's got umpteen animals in a dreadful state, and she needs to go into a home. This place hasn't got like this since yesterday, Tom. She clearly can't manage any more—the house is huge and it's falling down round her ears. Would you come and see her and try and talk some sense into her?'

'Sure. I've just finished my surgery, I'll come now,' he promised. 'Get her something to drink, and I'll be with you in ten minutes.'

She rang off and dialled the veterinary surgery.

'I'm sorry, Mr McWilliam's operating at the moment. Can I give him a message?' the receptionist said.

What could she say? 'Look, I don't even know if

I should be talking to him or if I should be contacting the RSPCA,' she confessed. 'I'm at Mrs Rudge's—'

'Oh, dear,' the receptionist said. 'Right, I'll get him to come round straight away. Someone told us her animals were looking neglected the other day, but we can't really do anything without her permission. I'll get him to come out straight away—he's nearly finished operating now. He shouldn't be long. What is he coming to see?'

'A pony, several cats and two dogs that I've found so far. I should be here some time.'

'Fine. I'll send him as quickly as possible.'

She put her phone away, took a deep breath and went into the house. Mrs Rudge was looking ashen, two blobs of red the only colour on her withered face, and Ruth squatted down again beside her and took her hand.

'Are they all right?' she asked wheezily.

Ruth shook her head. 'Well, sort of. They're hungry and they look ill, Mrs Rudge. It's just all got too much for you, hasn't it, my love?'

The woman's lids slid shut and fat tears squeezed out round them. 'I can't afford to feed them any more, and I can't get up—I've tried. Feed the dogs, dear. There's some dry food in the cupboard under the kettle.'

Ruth opened the cupboard and a rat scuttled out of sight. Dear God, whatever next? she thought with desperation. The dried food was a basic variety, but the dogs didn't seem to care. They whimpered and pushed at her hands, and she scooped out the last of it and put it in their filthy dishes.

Then she made tea for Mrs Rudge, but couldn't

bring herself to have one herself. It was black, of course, because there was no milk, but it was hot, and it was liquid, and that was the most important thing.

'Thank you, dear,' the elderly lady said with pathetic gratitude. 'I was so worried about them all.'

'And what about you?' Ruth said gently, rubbing her arm in slow, reassuring strokes. 'Mrs Rudge, you can't stay here like this. You need to be cared for.'

She shook her head. 'I'll do.'

Ruth gave up. Let Tom deal with her, she thought. Tom and Mac, whenever he got here and saw the state of the animals. She didn't even know if he could do anything—there was the question of cost, for one thing. Mrs Rudge clearly didn't have any money to spend on extensive veterinary treatment.

Please, God, don't let them all have to be destroyed, she thought sadly. It would break the old lady's heart.

CHAPTER SEVEN

'HAVE you got any clean sheets?' Ruth asked Mrs Rudge.

'In the linen cupboard on the landing,' she said, 'but mind the stairs. They're a bit rotten in places.'

She nodded, and opened the door to the hall. The air was musty and smelled of mildew and damp, and she didn't hold out much hope for the linen. She went up the sweeping staircase with caution, testing the steps and staying close to the wall. At least that seemed fairly solid!

She found the linen cupboard, but the sheets were covered in thick green powder and there was something interesting growing on one of them. It could have been a dead rat.

She closed the door fast, empty-handed. Cleaning Mrs Rudge up was a fruitless task if she had to put the sheets onto that urine-soaked bed. The only thing that would make any difference was a new mattress. She glanced in one of the bedrooms, but the roof had leaked over the bed and the mattress was ruined. Another bedroom had no bed in it, and there was a scuttling noise as she pushed open the door.

She gave up and went back downstairs. 'Sorry, they were pretty wet and horrible—I think there's a leak over the cupboard.'

'Be a miracle if there wasn't,' Mrs Rudge said wearily. 'I'm sorry. I was worried about you up there.'

A car drew up outside, and the dogs barked furiously.

'Bruno, Rufus, stop it!' Mrs Rudge ordered in a feeble, quavering voice. They didn't hear her, but Ruth went to the door with them and stroked them.

'It's all right,' she murmured in a calming voice. 'He's a friend.'

Tom raised an eyebrow. 'I am?' he muttered. He eyed them nervously. 'Good boys. Don't eat me, I don't taste nice.'

'Just now I think they're full,' she told him with a smile, then dropped her voice. 'She's in bed in the corner—I don't think the sheets have been changed for weeks. She must have come back last night and got straight back into the dirty ones—and they really are. They're vile. I didn't think there was any point in trying to clean her up, there's nothing in the way of linen—Tom, it's tragic.'

'I know. I'll talk to her. It can't go on.'

She wouldn't shift, though. No matter what either of them said, it seemed that Mrs Rudge would never give in to their persuasion—and then Mac arrived and appeared in the doorway.

'Hello, Mrs Rudge. I'm Andrew McWilliam—the vet. I think you know my father.'

'Of course.' She peered at him. 'I remember you—you used to come out with your father when you were a boy.'

He smiled and came into the room, crouching down beside her. 'I did, you're right. I remember you well. I'm surprised you remember me, though, after all these years.' He took her hand and squeezed it gently, and his eyes were compassionate and hugely kind. 'I gather things have got a little too much for you.'

She seemed to crumple. 'I've done what I can, but I'm so tired now,' she said tearfully. 'The cats keep breeding, and the pony, Freddie—he's a good boy, but I can't look after him. The fence is broken and I can't turn him out, and I can't afford the farrier any more, and his feet need trimming. I promised my granddaughter I'd look after him, and I can't let her down—not now she's gone—'

'Don't you worry about the animals,' he said firmly. 'I'll go and see what needs to be done.'

'You won't—you know...'

'Not without asking you, and not unless there's no other choice.'

'I've got no money,' she warned him.

'Don't you worry about that. I'll just take a look at them for now.'

She nodded, and with a brief smile Mac left the room.

'He'll look after them, won't he?' Mrs Rudge said wearily. 'He always was a good boy.' She turned to Tom and sighed. 'You're right, I can't manage. The house is falling down—sometimes I think it will, and then I won't have to worry any more. I've got nothing to live for since Clara died. Nothing.'

'Let's get you into hospital again and get you sorted out, and we'll let Mr McWilliam worry about the animals, shall we? And we can worry about you and getting you well again.'

'I'll never see them again,' she said tearfully, reaching to stroke the dogs who were lying on the bed at her side. 'Where will they go? Who'll have my boys?'

Mac came back into the room at that moment, and after a flicker of hesitation he went over to Mrs Rudge. 'The pony needs urgent treatment. I'm going to take him home with me now and nurse him at home, and I'll take the dogs, too, if you like. They need help as well—one of them's got a bad leg.'

'That's Rufus. He must have hurt it while I was in hospital. What about my cats? What will happen to them?'

Mac sighed and took her hand. 'One or two are very old and sick. I think they really need to be put to sleep, don't you, so they don't suffer? There's a grey one—long haired. She's very thin.'

'That would be Minnie. She's nearly twenty, poor old girl. All right,' she said with a quaver. 'Who else?'

'A black cat—very wary. Don't know if it's male or female, but it's got a damaged eye and jaw that looks very nasty. And a ginger tom. He's got a very badly damaged leg—I think he's been hit by a car. I don't know if I can save them. If I can, I will, but you'll have to trust me. The others are just thin and wormy, and I'm sure they can be found good homes in the area. You have to sign them over, though, to one of the welfare organisations. Shall I write something out for you to sign, and give it to them?'

She nodded. 'Would you? It breaks my heart, but I can't make them suffer. We're all here struggling for their sakes, and if it's not doing them any good, there's no point in going on,' she said weakly. 'I'm just so worried about paying—'

'Don't worry about that. The animals' welfare is more important than the money.'

She nodded. 'Thank you. I'll leave it all up to

you—you sort it out for me, Andrew. You're a good boy. Your father should be proud of you.'

And with that, she closed her eyes and sank back against the pillows, exhausted.

Minutes later she was on her way to hospital, the letter signed, and with a sigh of relief Ruth left the foetid, stinking room for the sweet-scented air outside. She chatted to Tom for a moment, then he left and she went round the back to look for Mac, to tell him she was going.

She found him in the first yard with the pony, trimming his feet with a farrier's knife.

'Poor little bastard,' he was muttering. 'What's going on, eh, Freddie? Whoa, lad. Stand up. Easy now, I'm nearly done.'

He put the foot down and straightened, and immediately Ruth could see the difference. The untrimmed one had a long, curving toe, looking almost like the curving slippers of the Middle East, the other was much shorter, looking more like a proper hoof, although it was grossly misshapen still.

'I'm just doing this so I can walk him into the trailer,' Mac explained. 'Would you like to talk to him while I do it? He's finding it a bit of a strain to stand on three legs, aren't you, son?'

She thought of her list of patients waiting for her, and shrugged. She'd get there. A few more minutes wouldn't make a lot of difference, she was already well behind. 'Will you be able to save him?' she asked, stroking his soft muzzle sadly. 'He's so painfully thin, poor boy. Can't you turn him out into some nice long grass?'

'No. He'll get laminitis—a painful disease of the hoof. He needs time to acclimatise to grass slowly, starting with a few minutes a day. I'll have to build him up very gradually. The first thing he needs is fluids. I've given him a drink, but I don't want to shock his system with too much cold water all at once.'

'Do you want me to put the kettle on?' she offered, but he shook his head.

'No. I'll give him warm drinks with electrolyte replacement in when we get back, and a nice soft bed in a stable with a foot of shavings on the floor so he can lie down in comfort. He'll think he's died and gone to heaven. How are the dogs?'

'Whining and unsettled. They don't understand where she is—they're standing at the gate.'

He finished trimming the second hoof and straightened. 'How long was she in hospital, do you know?'

'Three days, apparently. She discharged herself.'

'Silly old fool,' he said with affection. 'She lost her granddaughter—I don't know if you remember. She had a riding accident. She would have been a few years older than us. She had internal injuries, and she came round for a while and then relapsed and died. She was riding Freddie at the time of the accident, I believe, and she made Mrs Rudge promise to look after him, because her mother was going to have him shot.'

'And she's had him ever since. I do remember, we were at the same school—I must have been about twelve at the time, and Clara must have been fifteen.'

'That's right. It was tragic. Her parents were devastated and they were talking about having him put down, but my father refused to shoot him—I remember he managed to persuade them to let the pony live so long as nobody ever rode him again.'

'So he ended up here, with her grandmother,' Ruth finished for him. 'Clara would be gutted to see him like this,' she added, rubbing his face and cheeks. 'Poor old boy.'

'Old is right. He's probably nearly thirty. He was no spring chicken then, I don't think. I'll ask my father the next time I speak to him. He was their vet and Mrs Rudge's vet, too, I seem to remember. He'll know. He never forgets a case.'

Freddie rested his head against Ruth, and she rubbed his ears gently. 'How are your parents?' she asked him. 'Enjoying themselves in Australia?'

'Finding it hot,' he said, straightening up from the third hoof. 'They aren't brilliant with too much sun—I think they're ducking in and out of the shade, but Alec's house is air-conditioned, so they're all right.'

'It must be so strange to have a hot Christmas. Turkey sandwiches and rum and raisin ice cream on the beach. Bizarre.'

Mac chuckled. 'I could learn to cope with it. My hands are freezing in this wet mud. All right, boy, nearly done.'

She watched as he finished paring the last hoof, and then he straightened and stretched his back out. 'I could never be a farrier,' he said with feeling. 'I wasn't destined to spend all day like a duck with my head down and my tail in the air. Right, little man, let's see if you can walk.'

He took the lead rope from her and urged the pony forward a few steps, but it was a slow and painful process. 'He's a little better. They've been out of shape for so long it's put intolerable stresses on the joints of the lower leg. The trouble is, on that soft ground there's nothing to wear them down, and nothing to eat but what she's given him. Native ponies move about and travel miles over rough ground, wearing their hooves down. This little chap, I think, might be half thoroughbred—he certainly didn't look like this in his prime, did you, mate?'

The pony whickered softly, and Mac rubbed his nose and laid a gentle hand on his neck, stroking it quietly. 'Soon have you sorted out, Freddie. Don't you worry.'

'Are you going to get a trailer?' she asked.

'I was. I'll leave him tied up in here—he can't go anywhere anyway. I'll take the dogs with me now. Are you going on to your next patient?'

She looked ruefully down at her muddy foot. 'After I've gone home and cleaned up a bit. I'm way behind—I might ring the surgery and ask for some back-up, because this has taken much longer than I've got.'

A quick frown creased his brow. 'You should have said something—I'm sorry, I didn't even think.'

'Don't worry,' she said with a smile. 'They're all God's creatures, human or otherwise. I'd better go now, though. I'll see you later—can I pop over this evening and see how Freddie's getting on?'

'Sure. Stay for supper,' he suggested.

'That would be nice,' she agreed, and then belatedly she remembered that she wasn't supposed to be seeing so much of him.

Funny, that!

*   *   *

It took him ages to persuade the pony to load. Freddie had no strength, and yet he managed to resist all efforts to talk him into the trailer. In the end Mac did it with bribery—carrots and a few pony nuts in the bottom of a bucket.

The moment Freddie was in and munching, Mac whipped the tailgate up and fastened it, then climbed into the Discovery and drove slowly home. The two dogs and the ancient and injured cats were already at the surgery under observation, and he was going to take Freddie home, settle him in the stable for a rest and then go and operate on the cats.

'And God knows who's paying for this,' he mumbled to himself. Still, he could worry about that later. He'd made an oath when he'd qualified, but even so, he couldn't have walked away and left them without help. He was no saint, but he did need to be able to live with himself and sleep easy in his bed at night.

He'd just look on it as a prescription for sleeping pills.

He drove slowly—ridiculously slowly, with his hazard flashers on—but even so by the time he arrived home the pony was down. He took the central partition out to give him room to move, and eventually Freddie staggered to his feet and walked unsteadily out of the front.

The stable was ready, with warm water in an insulated bucket, a small hay net and a huge, deep bed of shavings to lie on. Not straw, because the hungry pony would have eaten it all and made himself ill, and he didn't need colic to add to his problems.

'OK, mate?' Mac asked, rubbing him gently behind his ears. 'I'll see you later.'

He put a lightweight rug on him to warm him up, then left him in peace, unhitched the trailer and drove back to the surgery. He could hear the howling even before he opened the car door.

'Those dogs are driving everyone mad,' Vicky, one of the receptionists, told him with a wry smile. 'You might want to sedate them.'

'I'll take them home once I've given them a thorough going over and treated them. How are the cats?'

'The black one looks like a goner,' she said softly. 'That eye is really awful, and the jaw.'

He nodded. 'It might be a tumour—sometimes they start in the jaw and push the eye out of the socket. I agree, I don't think there's anything we can do for it. What about the ginger tom?'

'He's hissing and spitting at everyone, but I think he looks fairly well apart from the leg.'

Mac nodded. 'I'll go and see them. Can you take me off the surgery list this afternoon? I'll have to deal with them, and I need to get back to the pony.'

He went into the back and started work. The first thing he did was put the black cat out of its misery. He'd been right, it did have a tumour. A great lump of deformed bone was cutting off its air supply in its nose, making the eye bulge and pushing the mouth open. It must have been suffering for months.

Then he tackled the ginger tom—tackled being the operative word. In the familiar surroundings of the farm it had been reasonable. Here, in this strange place with all the strange smells, it was terrified and quite beyond placating.

In the end he had to get one of the nurses to hold the hissing, spitting cat with gauntlets while he jabbed it with a sedative. They gave it enough to knock out a large dog, and in the end it sagged over and gave up the fight.

Then he could look at it. The leg, a back one, was broken in several places. They X-rayed it and it was irretrievable. It was obviously a fairly old injury, and it was badly infected. Mac hesitated. What did he do? Did he put the cat down, unsocialised and bad-tempered as it was, or did he give it a chance?

'I'm going to amputate,' he said without really registering his decision. The veterinary nurse gave him a look as if he were mad.

'You are? Why not just put it down? It's a horrible cat,' she said, sucking a scratch on her arm.

'Personality doesn't enter into it. We can't just refuse to operate because we don't like them, Sam. Animals are no different from people.'

She raised an eyebrow, but said nothing, and they operated on the leg, removing it at the hip and suturing the skin neatly back over the hip bone. Cats didn't miss their back legs nearly as much as their front, and once he'd recovered he'd soon be climbing and jumping again.

If he could find someone to feed and care for him. While they had him under anaesthetic, Mac castrated him as well to remove some of his less desirable tendencies, and then he was put back into his cage on an antibiotic drip to recover.

'Right, little Minnie,' he said gently, and lifted the elderly grey cat out of her cage. She purred and snuggled up against his chest, and he sighed and stroked her. She was so bony it was awful, but she seemed quite well. 'Let's have a look at you, little one,' he said kindly, and put her down on the examination table.

In fact, she was well. She was just thin, but he could find no other sign of disease apart from worms. There were no grounds to put her down, and maybe she could go to the nursing home with Mrs Rudge and lie on her lap all day. After all, there was plenty of equity in the house and land, tumbledown though it might be.

He'd bet his bottom dollar that it was a listed property, and that buyers would come flocking. There never seemed to be any shortage of crazy people that liked a challenge.

Him included. Not that he'd buy the house, but he had a sinking feeling about all the animals.

He wormed Minnie, gave her a vitamin injection and put her back in her cage, still purring contentedly. She was a little sweetheart, and if Mrs Rudge couldn't have her, then he was sure he'd find a corner somewhere for her to curl up.

He paused at the ginger tom's cage. Ex-tom, he corrected himself. 'Hello, Tripod,' he said quietly. 'How are you doing, mate?'

The cat was still out. He left it and checked the dogs, and found them pacing restlessly. They hadn't stopped howling since he'd got there, but when he came into sight they broke into a volley of barking.

'Hush, hush, boys, it's all right,' he murmured. He crouched down by the cage and put his hands against the mesh, and they licked them nervously. 'Good boys. It's all right. All a bit confusing, isn't it? Right, Rufus, let's have a look at your leg, boy.'

He opened the cage and they ran out, and he took them together into the examination room. Bruno was fine apart from being badly underweight, but Rufus had gashed his leg badly on something sharp and it needed cleaning and debriding under anaesthetic before it was stitched.

He shut Bruno away and took Rufus, protesting and howling, back to the operating theatre. He was very nervous, but quite gentle, unsure of his role now that he didn't have a mistress to protect, and he trustingly allowed Mac to shave his leg and inject him with the anaesthetic.

Sam looked at him over the dog's body as she adjusted the anaesthetic machine and monitored him. 'I suppose you're going to keep them all?' she said drily.

He shot her a grin. 'What on earth gave you that idea?'

'The fact that you've given that awful cat a name? Anyone else would have shot it on sight.'

'You're a hard woman,' he said with a chuckle, and cleaned up the infected skin and muscle around the cut. 'This is a mess. I'm going to have to put a drain in—he'll love that.'

'Pulling it all to bits will give him a reason for living,' Sam said, deadpan. 'Why don't you bandage the other dog, too? They can't howl when they're busy pulling bandages off. I'm sure we'd all be grateful.'

Mac laughed. 'I'll take them home—there are kennels at the house, and we haven't got neighbours. They can howl there to their hearts' content.' And probably will, he thought heavily. Andrew McWilliam, you must be mad.

'How are they all?'

Mac rolled his eyes, and Ruth thought she saw a

glimmer of despair in them. 'All right, I suppose. I seem to have acquired a three-legged cat, two dogs and a pony at a stroke.'

'Did you put the other cats down?' she asked, feeling sorry for the little grey cat who had done nothing other than grow old.

'No. The black one I did—it had an inoperable tumour. Minnie's all right, she's just elderly. I thought, if Mrs Rudge goes into a home, she could have her as a companion.'

'And until then?'

Mac smiled and led her into the little snug off the kitchen. There, beside the wall that backed onto the Aga, lay Minnie, curled in a ball inside a little cat bed, fast asleep.

'What do your parents' cats think of her?'

He shrugged. 'Not much. They took themselves off in a huff. They'll get used to it. It's not exactly the first time. It's how they've all ended up here, after all.'

He straightened up and looked her in the eye. 'This is your fault, you know,' he told her morosely. 'For the last four years, since I qualified, I've managed to avoid acquiring any pets. And now, suddenly, in one day, I seem to have five—and one of them's a pony, for God's sake! Now how do you account for that?'

Ruth smiled. 'I always knew you were a good man,' she said laughingly.

'Did you? Thanks for warning me. I thought I was a hard bastard. It comes as a shock to find I'm as soft as you and Mrs Blewitt. Come and have some supper—it's nothing exciting. I threw some jacket potatoes in the oven, and there's bacon and eggs and mushrooms in the fridge. I thought we could have a fry-up.'

'How healthy,' she said with a grin. 'Grilled, of course.'

'Absolutely. The oil's on the side.'

He set a heavy pan down on the hot plate, slopped oil into it and pulled half the contents of the fridge out. 'Bacon, eggs, mushrooms, tomatoes, sausages from the butcher because I caught his dog and took it back—that do for a start?'

She laughed and put the kettle on. 'I reckon it'll do. Shall we have tea?'

'No—I fancy a glass of wine. Probably a bottle, actually. I don't have to go out tonight, and I'm damned if I'm going to stay sober so I have to lie awake all night and wonder how I came to be so stupid.'

She laughed at him again, and gave him a hug. 'You're a good man, Andrew. Don't beat yourself up over it.'

He looked down into her face, and something deep and unfathomable happened in the cobalt depths of his eyes. Without a word he lowered his mouth and kissed her tenderly, cradling her against his chest and holding her like fine china.

It was a million miles from their passionate embrace here in this very kitchen less than a week ago, and yet it many ways it moved her more. She sighed and shifted against him, and he groaned and deepened the kiss. It was still gentle, though, still restrained, and when they drew apart she was shaking all over.

'Wow,' she said softly, and he gave a wry, twisted smile.

'Wow, indeed.' He studied her face for a second, then his eyes skidded over her shoulder and settled on the frying-pan. 'Oh, hell,' he muttered, and, reaching round her, he drew the pan off the hob.

She turned and looked into it. 'I like my bacon crisp,' she said with a grin. 'But perhaps not quite that crisp.'

He lifted it out and put in the sausages, then while they cooked he nibbled the shrivelled bacon and sipped the tea she gave him despite his protests.

He drank it anyway, and when he dished up he opened a bottle of red wine and offered it to her.

'I'm driving,' she reminded him.

'You could always stay.'

She shook her head, refusing to be tempted. 'I've got the animals at home—and, anyway, we aren't doing that.'

'We don't have to do anything,' he said, and she remembered her thoughts the night before, and how she'd wanted him there just to hold her.

Was it possible he was feeling the same way about her?

CHAPTER EIGHT

IT OCCURRED to Ruth on Friday that she didn't have a ball gown. Marvellous. She had a full day ahead of her, no prospect of any time to dive into town and go shopping, and, anyway, she didn't have any money to spare for such frivolities, not with the woodworm treatment to pay for any minute.

She sighed heavily, and Carol, one of the practice midwives, glanced across at her from her desk. 'You sound a bit weary.'

'Not weary,' she corrected, 'just in a bit of a quandary. I need a ball gown for tomorrow—I'm going to the Young Farmers' Christmas Ball, and I literally haven't got anything even slightly suitable.'

Carol eyed her thoughtfully. 'I've got a dress—it was too small for me really when I bought it, and I've only worn it once. I'll never get into it again, not now I'm pregnant, but it's a lovely dress. Would you like to try it?'

'Love to,' Ruth said fervently. 'It must be better than my jeans, whether it fits or not!'

Carol chuckled. 'I'll pick it up when I go home at lunchtime—will you be in this afternoon?'

'I'll be passing through—or would you rather I picked it up from you this evening?'

She shook her head. 'I'll bring it in—and then if it doesn't fit, you can go to town tonight and look around. They're open late because it's so near Christmas.'

Ruth thanked her, then scooped up her notes and went out on her rounds. Hopefully today everything would be straightforward, unlike yesterday with Mrs Rudge. She was apparently settling in hospital and looked a little better with the oxygen they were giving her. By the time the antibiotics had kicked in, she would be much more like her old self, but she still wouldn't be well enough to go home again, she was far too frail.

It was a sad time in everyone's life, she reflected, when the realisation came that you could no longer cope alone. The trouble was, nursing homes were so expensive, and the elderly worried so much about whether they could afford it. They also hated losing their independence, and so much of it was fear of the unknown.

No wonder it was such a stressful and worrying time for them, but when you came to the end of the road, like Mrs Rudge, there was no choice.

She passed the end of Mac's lane, and wondered how he was getting on with Freddie the pony and all the cats and dogs. He was a saint—or a sucker, which was more likely.

It rang a few bells with her, too!

She checked her list of calls on the seat beside her, and turned into a close of new houses just outside the centre of the village. Her first call was to John Grainger, the man on peritoneal dialysis, who had been doing really well. This morning, though, she'd had a message from him to ask if she could drop in. She was surprised, not having heard from him for days, but he'd sounded quite agitated, the receptionist said.

He was waiting for her, hovering at the door, and

he drew her in and took her into the cloakroom. 'Look,' he said, without preamble, pointing at the bag of cloudy, murky fluid in the sink. 'I don't know what it is, but it's come out of the tube and it was really difficult to drain it—I didn't get the whole lot out, I'm sure. It's about half a litre down.'

She looked at the bag of effluent, and nodded. It was full of strings, little strands of jelly-like material that hovered in the fluid. 'Fibrin,' she said. 'It looks like jellyfish—I expect it's clogging the tube. Not to worry, I'll inject a little heparin into the tube to clear it, and put some in the next few bags to keep it clear until it settles. It should be all right then, but if you have any trouble with the next bag, you're to ring me or the doctor, OK?'

He nodded, and she drew up some heparin and injected it into the end of the little tube that dangled from his abdomen. 'Once it's sloshed around a bit, it will sort itself out,' she said confidently. 'Don't worry.'

He smiled a little sheepishly. 'I thought that might be what it was, but it panicked me a little, seeing it for the first time.'

'I'm sure. Don't worry, you'll be fine. I'll take this other bag with me and send some off to the lab to check you don't have an infection. How's your weight? Fluid control all right?'

'I think so,' he said. 'I weigh myself full and empty and full again, to see if I manage to clear it all—I'm getting better at draining it. At first I found it quite hard to get it all out. I suppose it's finding the right position on the bed to let it drain.'

She checked his record card, and handed it back. 'You'll be fine. I think you're doing well. Are you managing to get some rest, or have you just turned into a workaholic?' she asked, remembering her last conversation with his wife.

He gave a wry laugh. 'Well, I have to say I'm probably still doing too much, but I have tried to cut down a bit. Linda's not threatening to leave me any more, so I suppose that's an improvement.'

'Certainly sounds like it,' Ruth said with a smile. 'OK, I'm off now, but, remember, any trouble with the next change and you must ring, all right? Leave it a couple of hours to let the fibrin dissolve, and then you should find it's clear.'

She went on to Martin Page, her blind diabetic, and found him and Katie both well and in good spirits. 'She's much better now, thank goodness,' he said. 'It's amazing how quickly they recover. The local representative from the guide dogs association came to see her—you know they own them, do you? I've only adopted her, I'm not allowed to own her.'

'Really?' Ruth said, surprised. She pricked his finger and squeezed the tiny drop of blood onto the test strip, then wiped it and checked her watch. 'Why's that?'

'So they can monitor the welfare of the dogs. There have been a few isolated cases of cruelty, apparently—people spending their feeding allowance on drink and then not feeding the dogs. That sort of thing. Seems crazy to me, how anyone could abuse their partner like that. Katie's my lifeline. I need her. I couldn't function without her, and there's no way I could expect her to work loyally for me if I mistreated her. It wouldn't be realistic.'

'No, I can imagine that,' Ruth said. Katie was sitting propped up against his legs, her head under his hand, and they were clearly devoted to each other. It was a real partnership, and one that she was sure brought Martin a great deal of comfort now he was alone.

'Well, that's fine,' she said, looking at the colour of the test strip. 'Right on target. Any other problems?'

'No. I'm fine. Here—this is from Katie,' he said, fishing around on the floor beside his chair. He handed her a box of chocolates. 'It's just a little thank you for bathing her stitches and looking after us both the other day.'

She took them and, without thinking, bent forward and kissed his cheek. 'Thank you,' she said softly. 'You're very kind. It was a pleasure looking after her.'

He flushed a little, and she wondered if he'd got the wrong idea. Please, no, she thought, but he hadn't. 'I hear you're going to the Young Farmers' Ball with the vet tomorrow,' he said with a smile. 'Enjoy yourselves, won't you? You both work too hard.'

'I'm sure it will be fun,' she assured him. 'I'll have to save the chocolates for afterwards, or I won't get into the dress!'

In fact, she fitted into the dress with ease. It was lovely, cut very simply in a rich ruby wine colour that gave her cheeks some colour and looked striking with her dark hair. Carol grumbled because she looked so good in it.

'I'm sure it never did anything like that for me,' she complained, and then gave Ruth a warm smile. 'You look gorgeous. I hope you have a super time.

God knows, you deserve it—it's about time someone took you out somewhere nice.'

'It's only the Young Farmers,' she said wryly. 'I expect it will just make us feel very old and sober and sensible.'

'No doubt. Try letting your hair down and behaving like a teenager.'

Ruth thought of the last time they'd behaved like teenagers, and managed to turn away before the hot tide of colour engulfed her. That night was going to haunt her. Had it really only been a week ago? It seemed much longer.

She went back to check Mr Grainger as she was passing later that day, and found his effluent had cleared, as she'd hoped. He was hugely relieved and much more relaxed.

She finished early, by a miracle, and went home, fed the dogs and cats, and drove over to the McWilliams' house to see how Mac was getting on.

She found him in the stable with Freddie, brushing him gently and crooning to him.

'Hi,' she said, leaning on the door and admiring the smooth, sleek muscles working under his shirt.

He turned and gave her a dazzling smile. 'Hello, yourself. How are you?'

'Fine. How are all your charges? Dogs still howling?'

He laughed. 'Sometimes. They seem to be accepting me. I'm feeding them up and trying to get them free of parasites at the moment. Rufus is still sore, but Bruno seems all right. Minnie's settled in—oh, I slipped into the hospital and saw Mrs Rudge, by the way. She looks a lot better, and I told her Minnie was still alive and waiting for her to go into a home so she could go and live with her, and she burst into tears. Poor old thing, she does miss them all.'

'I'm sure. I expect they miss her, too. How's the pony?'

'Better, I think. Seems a little steadier. He's very hungry, but he's basically all right. Once his stomach's settled down and is used to food again, he'll start to pick up. He was dehydrated as much as anything. I put a drip up this morning and gave him a couple of litres of saline. He seems to have picked up since then.'

'And who pays?'

He rolled his eyes. 'I have no idea. Me, I expect. Are you here for supper?'

She wasn't. She was here—why was she here? 'I thought I'd check on the animals,' she said, and wondered if it sounded like a feeble excuse to him. It certainly did to her!

He came to the door and kissed her over the top of it.

'You could stay,' he suggested, but she shook her head. She was supposed to be giving herself room, not finding excuses to see him.

'I've got a million and one things to do at home,' she said firmly, and let herself be talked into staying for a cup of tea.

They sat in the snug, with Minnie on Mac's lap purring like an engine, and before she allowed herself to fall prey to his charm and beguiling ways, she stood up and put her mug down. 'I have to go.'

'You said. Things to do. I won't get the wrong idea if you change your mind and stay for supper,' he assured her with a wicked twinkle, and she rolled her eyes and tried to stiffen her resolve.

'I'm going. See you tomorrow evening. Who's driving?'

'I'll drive, I'm taking you,' he said firmly. 'I'll pick you up at seven-thirty, all right? And don't forget it's usually a huge meal, so don't have too much lunch.'

'I don't usually have time for too much lunch,' Ruth said with a laugh. In fact, she didn't intend to give herself any time for lunch, because she wanted to finish as early as possible to give herself time to get ready.

In the end she got home at four-thirty, and she spent half an hour in the bath—which was as long as she could bear it because the room was so cold—and then dried her hair in front of the fire in the sitting room, with the television on and the cats and dogs all around her, leaning on her and clamouring for attention.

'If you put hair all over my borrowed ball gown, you'll be history,' she warned them all. She did her hair and make-up, but she didn't bother to put her dress on until she saw Mac's car coming from the bedroom window. Then she slipped it over her head, shimmied it down into position, wriggled her feet into her shoes and went downstairs, fending the dogs off and shooing them all into the kitchen.

She checked the fire guard, yelled, 'Come in!' to Mac, and then took a deep breath as she went back into the hall. Would he comment on her looks? Or would he say, 'Come on, woman, you're late,' or some equally flattering rejoinder?

He commented. Well, he didn't. Not really. He

just stood there, scanning her slowly from top to bottom and back again, then let out a low whistle. 'Wow,' he said eventually, and dragged in a breath and ran his hands through his hair, ruffling it.

He looked pretty wow himself, she thought. There was no doubt about it, men in evening dress did look good—and this one was superb. The blindingly white shirt was in stark contrast to the light tan he'd acquired from time spent outside, and the fit of the dinner suit showed off the breadth of his shoulders to perfection. He looked good enough to eat.

'Wow, yourself,' she said, and then firmed her voice. 'Come on, don't stand there gawping all night, we'll be late.'

'Tough,' he said bluntly, and pushed the door shut behind him. 'Come here. I want to kiss you.'

'I've done my make-up,' she protested, but he just smiled.

'Tough,' he said again, and bent and took her mouth in the gentlest, most achingly beautiful kiss she'd ever had.

'That's better,' he said, releasing her reluctantly. 'Now we can go.'

She nearly fell over when he took his hands from her shoulders. 'Do I need to put on more lipstick?' she asked distractedly.

He smiled. 'Not really. You won't keep it on long, looking like that. I may well have to stop and kiss you again before we get there.'

Her heart thumped against her ribs. 'Fine,' she said lightly. 'I'll take it with me, to be on the safe side.'

'Good idea.'

He settled her into the car beside him, and as they

set off, she thought idly that she could get used to this side of him very, very easily indeed...

The ball was loud, colourful and lots of fun. It was amazing how many people they knew, and, of course, most of them knew Mac's father, so there was no shortage of conversation in the quieter moments.

The food was wonderful, as usual, but Ruth was mean with herself and didn't allow her stomach to be ruled by her eyes. She didn't need to feel bloated, and the dress was too revealing—any little bulge would be all too clearly seen!

'Are you sick?' Mac asked, tucking in with a vengeance.

'No—just being restrained. I have had, as they say, an elegant sufficiency.'

He snorted and ate another forkful of rice and chicken. 'You're a nut. It's wonderful.'

'I know. I enjoyed it. I don't want to feel ill.'

Mac, however, had no such inhibitions and cleared his plate in record time. 'I take it you didn't stop for lunch?' she said drily.

'Or breakfast—and last night was pretty thin on the ground. I've been a little busy with my new charges, not to mention my father's little breeding herd that chose last night to start calving.'

She cocked her head on one side and studied him. 'Now you mention it, you do look a little tired,' she said sympathetically. 'Do you want to go?'

He shook his head and put his plate down. 'No. I want to dance with you in that sinfully sexy dress. Come on.'

He took her hand and led her onto the dance floor, then turned her into his arms.

'It's a fast one,' she said laughingly, and he grinned.

'That's OK, we'll halve the beat. Anything is possible.' He caught her hand in his, scooped it up against his chest and laid the other hand against the small of her back, drawing her closer.

It felt good. It felt better than good, in fact, it felt wonderful. She gave a tiny sigh, rested her free hand on his shoulder and relaxed against him. She could feel the strength and breadth of his shoulder under her hand, and against her other hand she could feel the steady beating of his heart. When he moved, his thighs brushed against hers, hard and solid, and with a low groan he eased her closer, so she was suddenly, shockingly aware of the fact that he was aroused.

For a split second she froze, and then she relaxed. Of course he'd reacted. She had, after all, so why not him? It didn't mean anything. It was all part of getting to know this side of him, and there was nothing threatening about it. Nothing she had to act on. She was safe here, in the crowd, and it gave her a sudden feeling of power.

She moved against him, chafing, tormenting, her actions concealed by the density of the crowd, and after another dance he turned her away from him, held her firmly against his front and propelled her towards the open French doors and out onto the terrace.

It was only a week before Christmas, and it was a cold, clear night, but it didn't matter. Once they were out in the darkness he turned her into his arms, sought her mouth and kissed her hungrily. She slid her hands round his waist under his jacket and snuggled closer, and he cupped her bottom and rocked against her with a tortured groan.

'Do you have *any idea* what you're doing to me?' he whispered against her skin.

'A fair idea. I suspect it's mutual.'

He lifted his head and looked down at her. 'How's this night going to end, Ruth?' he asked gruffly. 'Are you coming home with me, or is this just a wind-up?'

She felt a pang of anguish. She wanted him, of course she did, but it wasn't sensible. The sensible thing would be to go home to her own cold, lonely bed without him. Besides, it was too soon.

'I'm sorry,' she said with genuine remorse. 'I didn't mean to wind you up. No, I'm not coming home with you—not like that. Not for the night, Andrew, I'm sorry.'

'Still too soon, huh?' he murmured, and kissed her again, gently this time, regretfully. 'That's OK,' he went on, 'just so long as I know.'

For a while he held her, saying nothing, and then he eased away and looked down at her with shadowed, unreadable eyes. 'You must be frozen,' he murmured. 'Let's go back inside.'

He led her back to the dance floor, and she slid her arms round his neck, he locked his hands together over the small of her back and they swayed gently together till the MC called time.

Rather than putting her coat in the cloakroom and having to queue for hours to get it back, she'd left it in Mac's car, and he went to get it while she slipped into the Ladies' to tidy up.

Her hair, so elegantly piled on her head, was slipping down and made her look wanton and sexy. Her lips looked kissed, and in her eyes was a slightly glazed expression.

Arousal, she realised dimly. She swallowed and turned away from the mirror, hating herself for being unable to go with the flow and do what came naturally.

Even when they already had! She was a perverse and silly woman.

She went back out to the foyer, just as he came in with her coat. 'It's freezing, I'm afraid,' he said, 'but the heater's quick.'

Ruth shrugged into it, glad of the chilly fabric to cool her blood and bring some common sense back into her life. She felt drugged, OD'd on Mac. No, Andrew. Tonight, he was Andrew, not Mac. The person with her tonight was all man.

He escorted her to the car, seated her courteously and shut the door, then went round to his side and slid behind the wheel. Before he started the engine he leant across and dropped a kiss on her lips—a brief kiss, full of promise.

They said nothing on the way home, and Ruth's heart was pounding. It would be so easy for him to talk her into this. Just one well-placed word, the touch of his hand, the graze of his lips and she'd be there for him. She wondered if he knew how easy it would be, and hoped he didn't. Her pride needed some secrets.

He pulled up outside her house and got out, opening her door and ushering her inside.

'Coffee?' she asked, and he nodded.

'Thanks—that would be nice.'

Mac followed her through to the kitchen and found the animals all curled up asleep. The cats had broken into the airing cupboard again, but she didn't care. She couldn't think about anything except the look in his eyes and the touch of his hand.

'I'll put some wood on the fire,' he said softly, and went through into the sitting room.

She followed a few moments later with the coffee and found him lying on the hearthrug. 'You'll get covered in dog hair!' she protested, and he smiled.

'It's worth it. It feels lovely by the fire.'

'I know,' she said, and went and turned the cats off the spare quilt in the airing cupboard, then shooed the dogs back into the kitchen and shut the door. 'A quilt,' she announced with a smile, and he spread it out in front of the fire, sat down on it and held out his hand to her.

'Come on down,' he coaxed.

'Andrew, I meant it,' she began, but he cut her off.

'I know. I just want to hold you.'

She trusted him. Funny, that. It was about as sane as saying you trusted a fox in a hen house, but she did. She knelt down beside him, handed him his coffee and sipped hers.

'It's too hot,' he murmured. 'We'll come back to it in a minute.' He took her mug away, put it down and drew her into his arms with a ragged sigh. 'That feels good,' he whispered, and rolled against her, one solid, heavy thigh flung across her legs. It eased between them, rocking against her, and she felt heat shoot through her.

'Andrew, don't,' she whispered, and he smiled against her lips.

'Is that don't do it, or don't stop?' he asked teasingly.

'Either. Both. I don't know!'

He chuckled and moved his leg, settling down beside her and trailing an idle finger over her breast instead. Her nipple leapt to attention, and he flicked it gently with his fingertip, then, releasing her breast from the revealing neckline of her dress, he bent his head and closed his mouth hot and demanding over its tip.

She shuddered and made a strange noise, a pleading sort of whimper, and he lifted his head and looked down into her eyes. 'You are so beautiful,' he whispered, and kissed her again, paying homage to her with his skilful, clever lips.

'You said you wanted to hold me,' she whimpered, unbearably aroused and yet still not able to let go. She couldn't bear it to be trivial. Not now, not this time. Not the first time that they both gave their consent.

And now, suddenly, lying there in front of the fire in his arms, she realised what was missing.

He hadn't told her that he loved her, and without those few words, anything that happened between them was meaningless. She felt the need vanish, doused as if by icy water, and she struggled to sit up.

'Coffee,' she said with as much firmness as she could muster.

He lay there for a moment, just studying her, then with an understanding smile he sat up and reached for his mug.

'I think I just got my marching orders,' he said softly.

'I did warn you.'

'I know. I wasn't going to do anything more than that—even if you'd begged me. I want to be able to look you in the eye tomorrow, Ruth. That's more important than a quick roll in the hay.'

She sighed and ran a hand through her hair, belatedly remembering that it was still up.

'Let me,' he murmured, and, kneeling up behind her, he eased the pins out and sifted it through his fingers. It was unbearably erotic, and she just knew that he would be a wonderful lover. Slow, patient, gentle—her mouth dried and her legs felt weak.

Again.

'I need to go,' he said softly, and dropped a warm, teasing kiss on the sensitive skin below her ear. 'Don't get up, I'll see myself out.'

She stayed there—not because he'd told her to, but because her legs refused to work.

Traitors that they were, they would have been quite happy if he'd been less of a gentleman. She drank her coffee slowly, putting off the evil moment, then stood up, sorted out the fire and the animals, shook out the quilt and returned it to the airing cupboard, then went upstairs to her cold and lonely bed.

Fool that she was, she'd even changed the sheets, just in case, and in the end he'd been the one with the resolve! She slid between them, shivering and huddling up in a ball, and relived the evening.

He'd been wonderful—a real gentleman. He could dance superbly, he was witty and entertaining, he'd been thoughtful—and he was about as sexy as her blood pressure could take. Only one thing would have made it more perfect, she decided—if he'd told her that he loved her.

And Andrew McWilliam was a man who couldn't settle, a man with a nomadic past, a disastrous love life and no roots. He was here to cover for his father, and then would move on again, to another place, another practice—and another woman?

Would she be forgotten, brushed aside by the excitement of the moment? Maybe she was being hard on him, but what if he was a man like her father? He'd left her and her mother and gone off with another woman, after a whole string of affairs. He was on his third wife already, and the last thing—*absolutely* the last thing—Ruth needed in her life was a man like her father.

She'd be friends with Mac, she'd spend time with him while he was here, but she'd be wary—very wary—about getting involved with him. There was too much at stake.

CHAPTER NINE

RUTH drove past the end of Mac's lane several times next day, but she didn't go and see him. She wanted to—she even got as far as indicating as she was nearing the turning, but then she changed her mind and carried on. There was no point in being silly and, anyway, she was too busy to do more than pop her head round the door, and she knew she'd want to do more than that.

No, she had to have more resolve, she resolved. Much more resolve. Bucketfuls of it.

Last night hadn't helped, with her feeble brain dreaming about him all night and involving her in all sorts of things she'd have been better off not thinking about!

She resolved all day, and then, by seven o'clock, her bucketfuls ran dry and she got into her car and went round there.

The house was in darkness, except for the light in the back hall which she could see from the kitchen, and there was a light on in the stock barn beside the house. She followed the path round, and paused at the entrance to the barn.

'Hi,' Mac said, without turning his head. 'Bit busy at the moment. Can I help you?'

'It's me,' she told him.

'Oh, Ruth. Good. You couldn't go and put the kettle on, could you?'

Ruth studied him, up to the armpit as he was in

the wrong end of a cow, and wondered how it was that, bloodstained and smeared with unspeakable things, his hair rumpled and his clothes filthy, he could possibly look even more attractive than he had the night before in his immaculate dinner suit.

You need your head checked, she told herself.

'I thought all the hot-water thing was a myth?' she said.

'Not when you're desperate for a cup of coffee. Damn, I nearly had it—ouch, blast, don't have a contraction now!' He groaned and swore freely, resting his head against the cow's rump and muttering defamatory things about her ancestors.

'Are you all right?' she asked worriedly.

'No, I'm bloody well not all right!' Mac snapped, and then relented. 'Sorry. She just contracted down on my arm. It hurts like hell. And, yes, I'd love a coffee. Thank you, you're a darling. As quick as you like.'

He turned back to his midwifery. 'Right, you evil cow. Where the hell's that foot?'

She went into the kitchen and made a big pot of coffee, then dug around until she found a fruit cake that he was halfway through. That should fill a gap, she thought, and took the tin and a knife out with her.

'Here, grab this rope and pull,' he ordered as she went into the barn, and she set the coffee and cake down and helped him pull.

Feet appeared—little dark hooves—followed by skinny, knobbly legs and a soft pink nose, then with a great slithering rush the calf slid out and landed on the thick straw bed.

Quickly he released the rope from its feet, swiped

the membranes away from its face and pushed it towards mum. 'Here it is—a little heifer. Clever girl.' He patted the cow on the rump, and then backed off, shaking his head slowly.

'Never fails to get me, childbirth,' he said with a wry grin. 'Right, where's this coffee?'

'Down here. I brought you some cake as well.'

'Brilliant. Let me wash.' He sloshed water and disinfectant up his arm, rubbed it roughly dry with a towel and turned to her with a lazy smile that turned her world to mush. 'So, what brings you here?' he asked casually. 'Not that I'm complaining. I just wondered if you had a purpose or if you just came to give me the pleasure of your company.'

'Torment you, you mean,' she said with a rueful smile. 'I'm sorry about last night.'

His brow creased into a frown. 'Last night? What happened last night?'

She rolled her eyes. 'Don't be obtuse. I wound you up mercilessly. I just wanted to apologise.'

His brow cleared and he gave a lazy, sexy smile that did terrible things to her insides. 'Don't bother. I knew the score—and, anyway, I had the feeling it was mutual.'

'It was,' she confessed. She could feel a warm tide seeping up her throat, and she looked away from the searching gaze of those brilliant blue eyes. 'You must think I'm really stupid—I mean, one minute I'm all over you, the next I'm carrying on like a Victorian virgin—'

'Ruth, it's all right,' he said softly. 'Really. If it's going to happen, it'll happen in its own sweet time. There's no great rush. We'll wait till you're ready. Now, where's that cake?'

Ruth opened the tin and cut him a slab, and he demolished it in seconds. 'You haven't eaten again since last night, have you?' she said accusingly, and he gave a rueful smile.

'You guessed. I need a woman, you see—someone to look after me...'

'Yes, a mother,' she said drily.

Mac laughed and held his hand out for another slice of cake. 'Feed me, Mum. I'm starving.'

She slapped it into his palm, and he dropped one eyelid in a sexy wink that sent her heart into orbit and did horrendous things to her blood pressure. 'God, I love you when you're angry,' he said with a chuckle, and she had to turn away so he didn't see the foolish flash of hope in her eyes.

He didn't mean it, she told herself firmly. He didn't mean to say that he loves you. It's just a figure of speech.

'Do you want more cake, or shall I put it back in the kitchen out of the way?' she asked, without turning round.

'No, I don't want any more. I want you to stay for supper and spend the evening with me,' he told her.

She crumpled like a wet tissue. So much for her resolve!

He was going to get hurt. He knew that, just as he knew the sun was going to rise in the morning and the paper boy would be late.

He held out his hand to the snorting, wary horse and spoke softly, while the owner stood outside the stable door in safety and carried on a monologue of the horse's symptoms.

She was not an asset to the situation, he thought, and wondered why the horse hadn't killed her yet. He sighed. He was anti-everybody this morning, he admitted. The woman was probably perfectly nice, but he'd been up all night with another of his father's cows, and he'd finally got the calf out with a rope and pulley at four this morning.

He was exhausted, he could hardly see straight and all he'd had to eat since the ball had been the cake Ruth had fed him the night before and a scratch supper they'd thrown together. He wanted to crawl into a corner and sleep for a week, and this damned horse was going to try and bury him in the wall if he took his eyes off it for a moment.

'I've got the last vet's report here,' the woman was saying. 'He thought it was colic, but my horses don't get colic. I manage them far too well. I just thought I'd get a second opinion—you never can be too careful.'

He looked at the horse—the rolling eyes, the sweat breaking out all over its skin, the way it kept trying to go down.

'This horse has colic, I'm sorry. I'm going to have to give it a paraffin drench to see if we can move this obstruction through the gut. If that fails, he'll have to go to Newmarket for surgery. Could you come in and hold him so he doesn't go down while I get the gear?'

'Come in?' she said, eyes wide. 'But he's—'

Mac's antennae went on red alert. 'He's what?'

She looked shifty. 'He can be difficult in the stable,' she admitted uneasily.

'I'd noticed,' he said, wondering when she'd learned to be such a master of understatement.

'However, I'll need your help. If he's that difficult, we can sedate him a little—'

Did he understand? Or was it simply that Mac was distracted from the beast and gave him an opportunity? Whatever, the horse threw its head up, catching Mac's fingers in the headcollar. There was an audible crack, and then it swung its body round and slammed him broadside into the stable wall.

Pain, white-hot and searing, shot through Mac and he lashed out, punching it in the side with his thumb and giving himself a few vital seconds. 'Open the door!' he gasped, and threw himself at it, hurling himself through and slamming it behind him before the horse came back with his hooves to finish the job.

Not that there was much left to finish. He slithered down the door and fell in a crumpled heap at the woman's feet, and for a moment he just sat there, letting the waves of pain and nausea wash over him while the horse battered the door just behind his head.

'Are you all right?' she asked after a stunned moment, and he swore copiously and struggled to his feet. Was that concern in her voice for his well-being, or the likelihood of being sued? He decided he didn't much care. He just wanted to get away from that door before the damned horse came through it after him.

'No, I'm not all right,' he growled. 'I think my ribs might be broken, and at least one of my fingers. I'll call a colleague—he can come and see to the horse.'

He staggered over to the Discovery, teeth gritted, and yanked the door open. The seat seemed impos-

sibly high. With a resigned sigh he hoisted himself
up onto it with more pride than skill and dropped
his head back against the headrest for a moment,
letting the pain wash over him again. Gradually the
giddiness receded, and he turned on his mobile
phone and jabbed the buttons with his good right
hand. His left was useless, lying in his lap throbbing
painfully.

The surgery was engaged. He tried David's mobile number, and sagged back with relief when it
started ringing.

'Come on, come on, come on,' he muttered, but
there was no reply. In desperation he rang Ruth's
number, and she answered on the second ring. Relief
washed over him, almost taking his breath away.

'Ruth, I need you,' he said without preamble. 'I'm
up at Rickman's Farm at the end of that funny little
road that cuts through opposite the pub—know
where I mean?'

'I think so. I have a patient out that way. Is that
the odd woman with the horses?'

If he hadn't hurt so much, he'd have laughed.
'That's the one,' he agreed, his voice catching with
effort. 'I've been slammed against the wall and I
think I've broken my ribs and some fingers. You
couldn't come and rescue me, could you?'

'Oh, dear God. Do you need an ambulance?'

'No—just you,' he said unevenly. 'And could you
call the surgery? They're engaged—have another go
and ask them to send David. And tell him to sedate
the bastard. It's got colic, and the woman's a waste
of space. He might need an assistant.'

He ran out of adrenaline at that point, and sagged

against the door pillar, feeling bloodless and exhausted.

'I'll be with you in five minutes,' she promised,
and he let his eyes drift shut. Thank God she was
coming...

Ruth felt sick. All the way there her hands were
shaking, and she just hoped it was where he'd said
and that she could find him in time. Slammed
against the wall, he'd said. Just the thought of the
internal injuries he could have made her feel ill.

Thankfully she found it, and turned into the yard
to see Mac's Discovery parked beside the stable
block. He was in it, leaning against the driver's door,
and she went round to the passenger side and
climbed in, kneeling up on the seat and reaching
over to him, trying to force herself to be professional
and not just a hysterical woman in love.

Oh, dear God. What a time to realise!

'Mac? Mac, wake up,' she urged, resisting the
impulse to shake him. 'Mac?'

'I'm awake. I just hurt like hell,' he mumbled.
'Thank heavens you're here. Did you get hold of
David?'

'I phoned the surgery—I passed your message on.
You need to let me look at you—where do you
hurt?' she asked. It was quite obvious which hand
was damaged, from the awkward way he was holding it and the swelling in his fingers, but she was
worried about his ribs and wanted to know how alert
he was.

'Left hand,' he grated. 'And ribs—or collar-bone.
Whatever. It slammed me against the wall, the vi-

cious brute. I think it has a reputation—she wouldn't come in with me. That should have warned me.'

'Very likely. Where do you hurt most?'

He opened his eyes. 'Collar-bone, ribs, arm, fingers—take your pick. You name it, it hurts. I just want to go to bed.'

'You need the hospital,' she said firmly.

'Rubbish.'

'You need the hospital,' she repeated. 'Now, either I drive you there, or you drive yourself home.'

He gave her a malevolent glare, then shut his eyes. 'You're a witch, do you know that?'

'Yes. That's why they pay me so much—for nagging my patients. It's what I do best. Right. My car's beside you, so I'm going to come round and open that door, and you can get straight in.'

'I can't leave my drugs in the car unattended,' he said flatly. 'I'll have to drive.'

'Will you, heck.'

She looked over her shoulder at another car pulling in, and a man in green overalls got out of it and came towards them.

'Are you David?' she asked, and he nodded.

'What's he done?'

'*He* hasn't done anything—it's that bloody horse,' Mac growled. 'Watch yourself with it—I should dart the devil.'

'Or shoot it,' David said mildly. 'We've had trouble here before—is it black?'

'Yup.'

'It's uncontrollable. I'll talk to her, but I have to say I'm not in a hurry to go back in there. I've been kicked by it before. She can get it out and I'll treat it in the yard, but it hates being shut in. Are you going to hospital?'

'No—'

'Yes,' Ruth corrected swiftly. 'Could you take charge of all the drugs in his car, please, and take the keys back to the surgery with you and get someone to pick it up and take it home for him?'

'Sure. You look rough, Andy. Do what the lady says.'

Mac said something unprintable, and Ruth laughed. 'And you,' she said. 'Come on, let's get you out of here.'

Three hours later Mac was back in his bed, drugged up to the eyeballs and out for the count. He'd refused hospital admission, especially when he learned that his collar-bone and ribs were only bruised and not broken as he'd feared. Two fingers were broken after being trapped in the headcollar, and they were padded up and taped together to splint them. The rest of him, miraculously, had escaped injury.

Ruth gave him arnica to take to reduce the shock and bruising, and settled him in bed before giving him the painkillers. He went out like a light, and she sat for a while and watched him sleep and wondered what needed doing around the place.

She hardly dared put her head inside the barn, in case she discovered some obstetric anomaly that she was totally unequipped to deal with, but she found a pair of wellies and a jacket that fitted her by the back door, and went out into the yard to check that everything was all right. After all, she could always call a vet!

The barn was peaceful, the cows all standing quietly, the little calves suckling happily or curled up asleep on the straw. No imminent crises, then. Freddie seemed a little brighter today, too, watching her over the stable door with interest, and she rubbed his nose and gave him a tiny handful of grass from beside the barn.

'Your mum's getting better,' she told him. 'She'll be out of hospital soon—I expect we can bring her to visit you.'

He nuzzled her, looking for more grass, but, mindful of Mac's warning about laminitis, she regretfully denied him the pleasure.

The dogs out in the kennels seemed all right, and greeted her with wagging tails. Did they remember her? She wasn't sure, but they licked her hands through the mesh and seemed well enough. They had water, anyway, and she was sure Mac would have fed them before he'd gone to work. Thank goodness there was nothing drastic going on!

She went back into the house and made a cup of tea, then took it upstairs to watch Mac sleep. He was utterly crashed out, she realised, not only by the painkillers but with tiredness. There was another calf since last night—she wondered if its arrival might be something to do with his exhaustion.

The chair was hard. She shifted on it, then looked longingly at the huge expanse of bed beside him. He'd crawled onto one side of it, and the other side of the double bed was empty. If she sat very quietly on it, she wouldn't disturb him. She could prop herself up and read a book—it would be much better than sitting here on this hard upright chair for hours, and she didn't really want to leave him alone.

She found a book downstairs in the snug, and

went back up, slipped off her shoes and lowered herself carefully to the mattress. He didn't move, and after a moment she let go of the breath she was holding and picked up the book.

It wasn't that interesting, and she found her attention straying to him again and again. What was it about his lashes against his cheeks that made him look so innocent and vulnerable? His jaw was starting to show a little stubble already, and she could see the faint line of Thomas's scratch across the dark shadow.

She remembered the feel of that rough, dark jaw beneath her hand, and ached to touch him again, to hold him, to feel the solid, reassuring warmth of his body close to hers.

She glanced at her watch. Nearly six. Did the animals need feeding? She didn't want to wake him, but she felt she should. She was just reaching out her hand to shake him gently when his eyes fluttered open.

'Hi, there,' she said softly. 'How are you?'

'Sore. Thirsty.'

'I'll get you a drink and some painkillers. Do you want to go to the bathroom while you're awake?'

He closed his eyes for a moment, then nodded. 'Good idea.' He moved his arm, then bit back an oath and fell back against the pillows.

'Let me help you,' she said, already on her way round the bed.

'I can manage.'

'Yes, I know you can. You just don't have to. Don't be so stubborn.'

They managed the bathroom without too great a

loss of dignity, then she asked him what she should do about the animals.

'I'll come,' he said, and she fixed him with her best bossy glare.

'You will do no such thing,' she said firmly. 'Get back into bed. I'm not incompetent. Tell me what to do.'

For a moment she thought he'd refuse, but then he swayed against the wall and winced. 'OK. Get a pen and paper—I'll tell you.'

It took ages. Fork some silage to the cows. How much, for heaven's sake? Was there no end to the speed at which they could eat? They demolished each forkful as she gave it to them, and she sweated and struggled for nearly an hour.

Filling Freddie's hay net was another struggle. How full, and how on earth did you hold it open and shove hay in it at the same time? And then he needed water, and she had to fetch buckets, and then there were the sheep out the back that needed hay chucked over to them, and the dogs in the kennels needed food and water, and after all that there were the house cats and dogs to feed.

It took her till nearly eight, and then she realised she had her own animals to do at home, and Mac hadn't eaten anything.

'I'll go home and feed mine,' she told him, 'and I'll get a take-away, shall I?'

'Anything. I'm starving,' he mumbled. 'You're a love.'

Promising not to be long, she shot home, changed, hesitated a moment and then grabbed her overnight things, apologised to her confused dogs and cats and thanked God for the umpteenth time that her dogs were small enough to use the cat flap and had each other for company, and then headed for the door.

Supper.

The pub did meals. She went in, bargained for two portions of a hearty chicken casserole and went back to Mac's. She found some rice, threw it in a pan of boiling water, stuck the casserole in a pan on the low hotplate and went up to see him.

'All right?' he asked wearily.

Ruth nodded. She was exhausted from the unaccustomed physical work with the silage, her head was spinning and she was ready to put her feet up, but apart from that she was all right! 'Supper in five minutes,' she told him. 'I'll bring it up.'

He didn't bother to argue. She piled their plates, carried them up to the bedroom and ran down for all the other bits and pieces, and came back to find him picking at the chicken with his fingers.

'Patience is a virtue,' she admonished, handing him his fork, and he grumbled mildly for a moment—just until he got the first forkful into his mouth.

Really, you'd think he hadn't eaten in weeks, she thought, and then wondered when he had last eaten a proper meal. He'd lost weight in the past couple of days, she realised. Had he just been too busy to eat?

'Do you want anything else?'

He shook his head. 'Painkillers,' he amended. 'Just painkillers and a cup of coffee would be wonderful. My fingers are throbbing, and my shoulder's giving me stick.'

'How's the breathing?' she asked, the nurse in her belatedly coming to the fore.

'Careful,' he said with a wry grin. 'It's all right if I don't cough or laugh or sigh.'

'So you don't want me to get you a funny video to watch?' she teased.

He shook his head and gave her a crooked little smile. 'I just want to sleep, really. I'm so tired, and I hurt. I'll feel better in the morning.'

She doubted it, but he might be right. She gave him his next dose of medication and poured the coffee into him as he dozed off.

She took the debris down to the kitchen then checked all the animals, both out and in, one last time, before going back upstairs.

Ruth hadn't bothered to tell Mac she was staying, because he would only have argued with her, but she hesitated at his door. Should she sleep beside him, or in the room next door where she'd slept before?

She went into it, and found the sheets still on the bed. An omen? Or just a stroke of luck?

She undressed, washed quickly and slid into bed, then lay there, worrying about him. What if he had a slow internal haemorrhage that hadn't manifested itself earlier? If he went into shock, she wouldn't know.

'You're being absurd,' she told herself, and, punching the pillow hard, she turned on her side and closed her eyes. She didn't sleep. Not properly, at least. She dozed off a few times, and then woke with a start.

Mac, she thought, her heart pounding, and, throwing back the covers, she ran through to his room.

He was shifting restlessly, pushing the covers off

and muttering, and she knelt beside him on the empty half of the bed and laid a hand on his brow. It was hot and damp, and she eased the quilt away from him to let him cool.

'Ruth?' he mumbled.

She took his hand. 'Shh. I'm here,' she reassured him, and he made a small, sleepy noise and relaxed. She tried to get up a few minutes later, but his hand tightened on her wrist like a vice.

'Stay,' he said, his voice slurred.

As if she had a choice. His good hand was locked firmly round her wrist, and he wasn't letting her go anywhere. And she was freezing. With a little shrug, she squirmed under the covers and snuggled closer to him, and he let go of her wrist and slid his hand down to interlace his fingers with hers.

'You're cold,' he mumbled. 'Come here.'

She found her head snuggled on his good shoulder, his arm wrapped firmly round her, locking her against his side, and with a deep sigh he turned his head and kissed her.

He missed her mouth, the kiss landing somewhere between her nose and her eye, and he hugged her gently and sighed again. 'Love you,' he mumbled. 'Gorgeous—best thing that's ever happened to me. Sexy lady.' He gave a lazy chuckle and kissed her again, more accurately this time. He added something that could have been, 'See you in the morning,' and seconds later a soft snore drifted from him.

He's drugged up to the eyeballs, Ruth told herself. Drugged and sleepy and doesn't know what he's saying. She felt something wet on her face, and realised she was crying. Idiot. She scrubbed the tears away on the quilt and laid her arm carefully across his waist.

'I love you, too,' she whispered silently.

He grunted and turned towards her, throwing a heavy leg over hers and trapping her against him. She couldn't move. She didn't try. It was where she wanted to be, anyway, and in seconds sleep claimed her.

That was how she woke the next morning, to his body firmly pressed against her, his leg wedged between hers, and his eyes open just inches from her face.

'Good morning,' she said softly, and then mentally scanned her body. Her nightshirt was wound up round her waist, his hand was pillowed on her breast, and his legs—his very naked and masculine legs—were tangled with hers in a very intimate and compromising way.

'God, woman, you pick your moments,' he grumbled, and winced. 'I hurt like hell, my mouth feels like sandpaper, my fingers are about to drop off, and I wake up and find you here next to me, looking rumpled and sexy and good enough to eat. Except just at the moment I can't eat you, because I hurt too damned much. What a bloody waste.'

He closed his eyes and eased away from her, rolling onto his back with a low groan.

'Painkillers?' she offered.

'Painkillers, tea and a hot shower, in that order. And do me a favour.'

'Sure,' she said, expecting it to be a phone call or something like that.

'Get some clothes on,' he said in a gruff voice that she didn't quite recognise. 'I really, really don't feel well enough for a cold shower today.'

CHAPTER TEN

'YOU can't go to work!'

'I have to,' Mac growled, spooning cereal into his mouth and glaring at Ruth. 'I don't have a choice.'

'What can you do?' she asked practically. 'It took you hours to shower with one hand.'

'I can do enough. I can look at animals and diagnose.'

'And treat them how?'

He shrugged without thinking, and swore copiously under his breath, pain furrowing his brow. If the truth were told, he wanted nothing more than to crawl back into bed—preferably in her arms.

'And how are you going to get around? You can't drive—'

'Of course I can.'

She snorted. 'How will you change gear? Your Discovery isn't an automatic.'

'I'll manage.'

'Right. Superman strikes again. Well, I think you're an idiot. You were off your head on drugs half the night, talking rubbish, and now you get up and say—'

'Rubbish?'

She coloured. 'You were sleep-talking. Mumbling all sorts of things.'

He studied her face guardedly, desperately trying to remember what he'd said. 'About you?'

'Partly,' she admitted reluctantly. She looked as

if she'd wished she hadn't brought it up, and he had a horrible sinking feeling he'd made an ass of himself. 'I think it was proximity,' she added.

He gave a slightly strained laugh, remembering the feel of her body tangled with his. 'Very likely,' he agreed, trying to forget before he embarrassed himself. 'You were pretty proximal—or do I mean approximate? God knows. It would have been a miracle if I hadn't been talking about it.'

He stood up, thrusting his chair back and stomping over to the sink to dump his bowl. Damn, his arm hurt. 'Whatever, I'm going out to the surgery today, and if I have to struggle with dodgy fingers, so be it.'

'Not to mention the ribs and collar-bone and shoulder joint.'

'They're fine. You heard them at the hospital.'

'No, they just aren't *broken*. They aren't *fine*, by any stretch of the imagination.'

'You fuss too much,' he said flatly, and then couldn't manage to get into his coat. 'Give me a hand with this,' he said ungraciously. 'I need to do the stock.'

'I've done them. I gave the cows more silage while you were having your shower, and I've given Freddie a hay net and fed Bruno and Rufus and all this lot, and I've shot home and fed mine, too. It's all done.'

Mac stared at her in disbelief. 'How did you do all that?'

'I hurried,' she told him bluntly. 'Unlike you in the shower.'

Heat scalded his cheeks. He'd stood under the stream of hot water for ages, willing his body to forget hers, wondering how he could feel so damned awful and yet still want her. 'I wasn't that long!' he said, denying it to himself as much as to her.

'You were hours.'

'That was dressing,' he snapped defensively. 'Do you have any idea how damn difficult it is when nothing works and your hand is taped up like a sausage?'

'My point exactly,' Ruth said in irritation. 'That's why I don't think you should be at work. Will your clients thank you when you can't do the job they're paying you for? I doubt it!'

He glared at her. 'Why don't you just go to hell?' he snarled.

'What, and let you struggle alone? Who will that help? Certainly not the animals you're so concerned about—or is it just your pride that's on the line?'

He sighed and stared down at his feet, guilt swamping him. 'I'm sorry. You've done a lot for me and I'm being thoroughly ungracious. You should just tell me to take a hike.'

She put a hand on his arm, and he could feel the heat of it all the way through to his bones. 'I'm off today,' she told him softly. 'Would it help if I drove you?'

He met her eyes and noticed yet again what a beautiful green they were, soft and luminous, utterly forgiving, and he felt like a rat. 'You don't want to do that,' he protested half-heartedly.

'Take me out for lunch,' she said. 'As a thank-you.'

He nodded, giving in. He needed her help, there was no denying it. 'Sure. Do you need to go back to your cottage?'

She shrugged. 'Not really. We could go now, if you want.'

He nodded again. 'OK. Thanks. Um, could you help me with my coat?' he added, swallowing his pride.

She managed not to smirk, bless her heart. She probably wanted to, but instead she helped him into his coat, tied his shoelaces without a murmur and went meekly to the car, tongue still firmly in cheek. He didn't know whether to hit her or kiss her...

Mac had been grim all day, she thought later. He must have been in pain, but he'd struggled on, doing what he could, admitting defeat periodically and asking for her help or the help of the client.

He'd got by, but Ruth had the feeling he was glad when the day was over and he could fall into bed and relax.

He'd phoned the following morning to tell her that he felt much better. She wasn't sure if she believed him, but she had no choice. She was back at work after her two days off, and in between her patients she was giving her own pets some much-needed love and attention.

She slipped home at lunchtime to talk to them and throw a load of washing in the machine, and while she was there she had a phone call from the surgery, asking her to call in on Mrs Frayne on her way back.

'She sounds a bit rough—said she wasn't well. Can you pop in and see if Tom needs to call on her?' the receptionist asked.

Ruth glanced at her watch. She had a busy afternoon scheduled already, and if she carried on with her chores she'd just be late tonight.

'Sorry, boys and girls,' she said to the animals, and left them yet again. She let herself into Mrs Frayne's bungalow with her key, and found her in bed in a dreadful state. She'd been terribly sick, and she looked waxy and awful.

'Oh, you poor love. Whatever's happened?' Ruth exclaimed gently.

'So ill. Thank goodness you're here,' Mrs Frayne said, and started to cry weakly. 'Thought I was dying. Oh, I'm so sick…'

She retched again, and Ruth held her head and tutted, then cleaned her up a little and checked her pulse. 'Tell me your symptoms,' she said, noticing the racing pulse and the visible heartbeat through her nightdress.

'Headache—terrible headache—and sickness, and tummyache. Oh, my tummy's so sore.'

'Diarrhoea?'

She shook her head. 'Not yet, but I'm churning. Oh, dear, I do feel so bad.'

Ruth nodded. 'I think it's food poisoning. What did you have for supper last night?'

'Oh, I wasn't feeling very good, so I had a little piece of chicken left over from a roast—I just heated it up with a bit of gravy.'

'Chicken? That fits. My love, I think it's salmonella. You're very dehydrated—look.' She plucked a little pinch of skin on the back of Mrs Frayne's hand, and it remained tented up, sinking only slowly back to her hand.

'Oh, look at that!' she said in surprise. 'Why is it?'

'You need fluids, and you can't keep anything down. I think, as you're already so frail, you probably ought to go into hospital for a day or two just until you're better. I'll call Dr Carter and he can come and see you, and I expect he'll admit you straight away. I'll ring him.'

He did admit her, and Ruth called her daughter-in-law to let her know. Hopefully, as well as visiting her, they could clear up the bedroom and change the sheets so the house would be ready for her return.

She went home and changed her uniform, then carried straight on with her calls, only an hour behind by now. After the drama of the last two days, it was all she needed, but that was community nursing for you. Still, Mr Hubbard should be quick. His blood tests were back, showing an improvement in his anaemia, and she simply had to report that to him and tell him to keep taking the tablets.

If only life were so simple!

'I've gone stone deaf,' he told her as she went in. 'Just in the right ear. I don't suppose you'd like to syringe it for me?'

'What, so you can hear the gossip better?' she said, and had to repeat it.

'I'll get the things from my car,' she said loudly. 'Hang on.'

It only took a few minutes, and to their surprise a huge lump of wax was washed out, impressing both of them.

'That's better!' he said with a beaming smile. 'I'll be able to hear all about what you and that young vet are up to—I gather you were there again the other night.'

'I was—aren't you going to enquire after his health?'

'Two broken fingers and a few bruised ribs, I heard.'

'What, even with this lump of wax?' she said mildly, and contemplated ramming it back in to deafen him again. Pointless. He'd take up lip-reading.

The phone was ringing as she arrived home, and it was Mac, to tell her that Mrs Rudge had been discharged from hospital and was now in a nursing home in the village. 'I thought I'd go and visit her and take Minnie,' he said. 'I've spoken to the matron, and she thinks it would be a good idea. Fancy coming?'

She contemplated the three days' worth of chores she had to do, the neglected dogs and cats, and the pile of ironing growing steadily in the corner. Plus she hadn't yet written her Christmas cards or done any shopping, and there were only three more shopping days to Christmas.

'Sure,' she agreed with a silent sigh. 'Want me to drive you?'

'No, I'm fine. I'll pick you up—ten minutes?'

'Fifteen. I want to change,' she told him firmly.

She was ready when he arrived, waiting outside on the step, and she climbed into the car and threw him a smile. 'So how's the invalid? Mr Hubbard knew all about you, despite having a piece of wax in his ear that Madame Tussaud's could have made good use of.'

He chuckled. 'Nothing changes, does it? I'm fine. Much better, thanks. I've learned to do all sorts of things with two fingers and a thumb, and my shoulder's feeling better now. You'll be pleased to know the horse is fine after treatment, and David escaped unscathed.'

'I'm glad about David,' she said frankly, 'but I wonder about the horse. Shouldn't it be put down?'

He shook his head. 'It's all right. It's just bolshy. It needs a stronger owner, someone who can put it in its place without hurting it. It's just been allowed to get away with too much for too long.'

There was a miaow from behind them, and Ruth swivelled round in her seat and held out her hand to Minnie in her carrier behind them. 'Hello, sweetheart. You're going to see your mum.'

'Let's hope she likes it there,' Mac said thoughtfully. 'I suppose she could always come back to me if she doesn't. I've got Tripod now, the ginger tom—'

'Don't tell me. It's got three legs.'

He gave her a wry smile. 'You guessed.'

'Funny, that.'

They pulled into the car park of the nursing home, and Matron greeted them and showed them through to a lovely cosy little room on the ground floor, with French doors out into the courtyard garden. There was even a cat flap in the glass, courtesy of a previous resident's cat, Matron explained, so it was perfect. 'Such a stroke of luck that we had this room available—we don't often get vacancies,' she told them.

Mrs Rudge was sitting propped up in her chair, looking unbelievably ancient but nevertheless much better, and she looked at them as they went in and her face lit up.

'Minnie?' she said tremulously, and Minnie

squawked at her and clawed the paper in the bottom of the carrier, trying to get out.

'We'll close the door for a minute,' Matron said, and Mac opened the cat carrier and lifted Minnie out, putting her on Mrs Rudge's lap.

'There you are, old girl, back with your mum,' he said softly, and Minnie purred ecstatically and curled up on Mrs Rudge's lap, paws folded under, and dribbled in delight.

'Oh, it's so good to see her again!' the elderly lady said tearfully. 'I've missed all of them so much the last few days.'

'You're looking well,' Ruth said, surprised at how fast she'd rallied.

'I am well. Warm and comfortable, and my chest is much better. I'm so grateful to you both for all you've done. I hardly dare ask about the others—'

She broke off, obviously desperate to hear, and Mac told her about Freddie in his stable, and Rufus's leg healing, and Tripod's amputation, and the black cat being put down because of the tumour, and she nodded and teared up and closed her eyes.

'I don't know how to thank you, I really don't. I was in such a muddle, and the social worker has found me this lovely place, and once my house is sold I'll be able to pay all your bills. It's such a relief. What about the other cats?'

'They've all been caught now and taken to the Cats' Protection League for rehoming,' he told her. 'They won't be put down. Most of them will end up on farms, I expect.'

'Good. Thank you. Oh, Minnie, it is nice to see you.'

They stayed a while with her, and Mac handed

Matron the low-protein food the elderly cat needed to protect her kidneys from damage, and then they left the two of them alone to get reacquainted.

'That was a success story, anyway,' Mac said with a grin as they drove back to Ruth's cottage. 'And maybe, one day, my father will get paid for the treatment I gave them.'

'Looks that way,' she agreed.

He pulled up outside her cottage and cut the engine. 'I don't suppose you want to invite me in for a minute, do you?' he suggested with a coaxing grin. 'I wanted to ask you about something.'

'Sounds mysterious,' she said with a laugh, trying to stop her silly heart from working overtime. He didn't want to ask her *that*, for heaven's sake! She was getting romantic and stupid in her old age. 'Sure, come on in. The place is in chaos, but as it's your fault I shan't bother to apologise!'

Ruth turfed Thomas out of the ironing basket and Fluff out of the airing cupboard, and put the kettle on. 'Ask away, then. What is it?' she prompted impatiently, still struggling with the little flicker of hope that wouldn't lie down and die.

'I thought of having a few friends round for drinks on Christmas Eve, before midnight mass. My parents usually do it, and I thought it would be nice to carry on the tradition in their absence. I wondered if you'd like to help me.'

The flicker of hope was finally suppressed. 'Sure,' she said, amazed at the huge wave of disappointment that washed over her. 'What do you want me to do? I'm working on Christmas Day and Boxing Day, but I've got Christmas Eve off. I need to run

over to Mum's in the morning with a few presents
for them all, but other than that I'm yours.'

Something—possibly lust?—flickered in his eyes,
and found an answering hiccup in her heart.

'Sounds promising,' Mac murmured.

'Don't get over-excited,' she threatened teasingly,
wishing he would and that he'd sweep her off her
feet and tell her he loved her—now, while he was
sober and not under the influence of painkillers, instead of semi-conscious in the middle of the night,
so she didn't dare believe it.

'You're such a spoilsport,' he said with a lazy
smile, and she grabbed the kettle and made tea to
give her something else to think about, apart from
the power of that smile and how much she'd missed
him last night.

She'd only slept with him a few hours the night
before that, and yet in her bed in the wee small hours
of last night she'd felt desolate and alone. If only he
loved her—really loved her—and she dared to believe it.

'Tea,' she said, almost smacking it down on the
worktop beside him. 'So what do you want me to
do for this party? Make canapés?'

'If you feel like it. I thought we could have a few
nibbly things and some mince pies and mulled
wine—nothing flashy, just something warming before we all walk down to the church. You've been
before, haven't you?'

She nodded. 'I used to come every year, when we
were younger. It was always fun. Who are you going
to invite?'

He shrugged. 'The usual crowd—practice staff,
local farmers, Julie and Mike—anyone who's

around, really. My father does it as a sort of thank-you to his clients.'

She nodded. 'OK. I'll do some cooking on Saturday, then, if you like. Shall I do it at your house?'

'Makes sense. Do you want me to shop?'

She laughed. 'No. I'll shop. I'll know what to do to be flexible. Anyway, I've got to go shopping for me or I'll starve.'

They dreamed up a list of nibbles, and he went on his way, leaving her wondering if and when she'd ever get everything done before Christmas...

Mac was quiet. Very quiet, and withdrawn. Ruth piled the shopping on the kitchen table, tried not to remember that stolen moment of ecstasy they'd shared on its ancient and battered surface, and put the kettle on for something to do while she waited for him to speak.

'Is this everything?' he said tersely.

'I think so. I'll need baking trays and serving dishes.'

'In here,' he said, opening a big cupboard in the wall. 'Help yourself to anything you want. I've got things to do.'

'Fine.' She watched him go, shrugged slightly and swallowed the little pain his offhandedness had caused. He was obviously preoccupied about something.

She unpacked the shopping, then hard-boiled the eggs for the bridge rolls, washed cress, thawed prawns and made up mayonnaise, and made a huge batch of pastry for the mince pies. She worked mechanically, wondering what was wrong, if it was something she'd said or if it was him.

He came in and out periodically, getting the fires going in the drawing room and dining room, vacuuming the floors, plumping the cushions and extracting Tripod from behind the Christmas tree in the hall, decorating the tree—and all the time he was distant, remote, a little distracted.

'Have you heard from your parents?' she asked, wondering if it was something about them that was troubling him.

'Yes. They're fine. They send their love.'

Well, that was short and sweet! She gave up trying to make him talk and concentrated on her canapés, then just before five she went home to bath and change and feed her animals.

'I really will spend time with you soon,' she promised the dogs. 'Maybe tomorrow we'll find time to go out for a walk at lunchtime. Everyone's too busy on Christmas Day to call the nurse then.'

She tried not to think about Mac and why he was so offhand, but deep inside her a little chill of dread was building. Maybe he was warming up for the big brush-off?

But he said he loves me! her heart protested.

'And he was drugged up to the eyeballs!' she told herself crossly. 'Stop harping on that. It didn't mean anything. Face it, kid, he's got bored with you, and with the practice. It's all too home town and cosy for him. He wants the bright lights and the cutting-edge veterinary practice and the rich, swooning female clients—or client, at least. Not a community nurse who's as poor as a church mouse and overrun with aged animals needing attention!'

She put on her Christmas outfit—her long tartan skirt, her red jumper and her ankle boots, so she could walk up to the church without crippling herself in court shoes on the uneven road, and then, without allowing herself any more time to wallow in self-pity, she went round to Mac's.

The house looked lovely. It always seemed to do Christmas very well, somehow, and she'd spent many a happy festive hour here in her youth. Odd, how unfestive she felt today. Still, she thought, chewing her lip distractedly, it was only a few hours, and she'd promised him. She'd see it through, then she'd go without a fuss.

There was no point in getting upset, it wouldn't change anything.

Something was wrong. Ruth had been off with him all day, and the sick feeling in the pit of Mac's stomach kept growing. He saw his guests off at the door, promised to meet them in the church later, and looked around for her car. It was still there, wedged in the corner behind Mike's Land Rover, and he guessed she'd been unable to get it out.

So where the hell was she? He hadn't seen her for nearly an hour, and now, at the critical moment, she'd disappeared.

'Ruth?' he called, standing in the drive, listening. She wasn't about. She wasn't in her car, but her coat was missing. He'd checked on the way out. That meant she hadn't tucked herself away in some corner of the house.

He checked the barn, not thinking for a moment that he'd find her there, and out the back with Mrs Rudge's dogs. Not there, either. There was only one other place he hadn't looked, and that was Freddie's stable.

He opened the door, and there he found her, sitting on an upturned bucket with tears staining her face, the pony standing quietly beside her, nuzzling her shoulder.

'Ruth?' he said gently.

She looked up. 'I know. It's over. You want me to go. Well, I will, I promise, but I can't get my car out, so I'm sort of stuck at the moment.'

Her voice hiccuped and broke, and he sighed raggedly and pulled her to her feet. 'Why should I want you to go?'

She shrugged, and a tear slid down her cheek and splashed off his hand. 'Why wouldn't you? I'm no use to you, after all. You don't even like me.'

'I don't know what the hell you're talking about, but you're freezing to death out here and you need to come inside,' he told her firmly. 'Come on.' He wrapped his arm round her for support, and led her towards the door of the house. She came reluctantly, stumbling slightly on the uneven ground, shivering with cold.

'Silly girl,' Mac chided gently, leading her into the drawing room and shooing the dogs out of the way. He peeled off her coat, sat her down by the fire and handed her a glass of mulled wine. 'Here, drink this, it'll warm you up.'

'Why are you bothering?' Ruth asked woodenly. 'And, anyway, I can't drink this, I'm driving.'

'You're going nowhere,' he told her. 'At least, not until we sort this out. What's the matter with you? You've been quiet and preoccupied all day.'

'*I* have?' she said in evident surprise. '*You're* the

one who's been quiet! You've been mooching round
all day, looking hunted, and every time I've spoken
to you, you've nearly bitten my head off—either that
or you've ignored me! What was I supposed to
think?'

He stared at her, astonished, then thought back
over the day. Had he been preoccupied? Maybe he
had. He'd been nervous, certainly, dreading the moment he had to do this, fearing her reply, because
nothing had ever mattered quite so much and he
didn't quite know what he'd do if she walked away.

'I'm sorry,' he said quietly. 'I didn't mean to be.
I was just—afraid.'

'Afraid?' she said, her eyes widening. 'Afraid of
what?'

He shrugged, knowing that this was the moment
he'd been dreading, the moment when his life would
come tumbling down around his ears.

'Afraid that you'd say no,' he admitted. 'Afraid
that you'd laugh at me and tell me to go hell. I've
been looking for you for so long, and I haven't
known what I was looking for. Then I came back
here to cover for my father, and you were here, and
suddenly it all seemed so simple. I didn't trust it—
I didn't believe it could all be so easy, so straightforward, so obvious.'

He looked up, forcing himself to meet her astonished eyes, and carried on. 'I love you,' he said unevenly. 'I think I probably always have, but I just
didn't realise it. You were always so aloof when we
were kids, and then when I came back you still held
me at arm's length—until that night in the kitchen.'

'I didn't realise you were interested,' she said,
dazed.

'Of course I was interested—and doing my best to hide it, because I felt like a love-struck fool and I didn't dare hope you felt the same. And then, that night, when we made love—I was even more afraid, because I knew then just how much you meant to me, and I tried so hard to give you room, but then on the night of the ball I thought I was going to die if you didn't let me stay.'

He gave a short, cracked laugh. 'And you didn't, of course, and so I thought I'd hang on and give you more time, but I can't give you any more. It's tearing me apart. I need to know how you feel, Ruth— if there's any chance you'll ever love me—because somehow in the past few weeks you've become the centre of my world, and without you in it I don't know if I can go on. I love you.'

A slow, tearstained smile curved her lips, and she knelt up and reached out to him. 'Oh, Andrew,' she said softly. 'I never thought I'd ever hear you say that. I love you, too—so much. So very, very much!'

He caught her as she threw herself at him, and hardly noticed the stab of pain in his shoulder as he pulled her hard into his arms and kissed her as if he were dying for her.

He felt the heat kick in, felt the tension disappear like a broken watchspring, only to be replaced by tension of another sort, a slowly building fire that threatened to consume him.

He lifted his head. 'Not here,' he said gruffly. 'Not like this.' He stood up, drawing her to her feet, and led her upstairs to his bedroom. It was cold, but he had heat enough for both of them and plenty to spare. He undressed her slowly, carefully, releasing her hair and fanning it over her shoulders, catching his breath at her loveliness.

His own clothes disappeared in an instant, and then he drew her over to the bed and lay down, taking her into his arms. Her body was hot against his, in sharp contrast to the sheets, and she wriggled closer to his warmth.

'I'm still not on the Pill,' she warned, and he gave a ragged groan and dropped his head against her shoulder.

'Would it be such a tragedy to have my child?' he asked unsteadily. 'I'll stop, if you want—'

'No! No, I don't want you to stop. I'd love to have your child,' she said gently. 'In fact, it's quite likely to happen if we make love now.'

A huge lump grew in his throat, and speechlessly he lowered his mouth to hers. 'I love you,' he whispered after an endless moment. 'I love you...'

She'd been right. He *was* a wonderful lover. Slow, patient, generous, emotional—he'd taken her higher than she'd ever known it was possible to go, and afterwards, when she'd cried, he'd held her close, so close that she couldn't tell where her tears ended and his began.

Would they have a child? She couldn't think of anything that would make her happier, apart from more time alone with him first to enjoy him and get to know him even better.

There was only one thing missing—

'Can you reach my trousers?' he asked.

She peered over the edge of the bed, and nodded. She stretched out an arm, and he locked his arm round her waist as she leant out of the bed, pulling her back with a laugh as she threatened to tip off the edge.

'Here,' she said, and he took them and slid one hand into the pocket and pulled out a little blue velvet box.

'I don't know if it'll fit and, now I think about it, I haven't even asked you if you'll marry me,' he said with a slightly ragged laugh.

'Yes,' she said with a smile, wondering if he'd read her mind. 'Yes, I'll marry you, Andrew, you know that.'

His smile faltered. 'I don't know. I hope, but I don't know.'

'Well, you do now,' she said, raising herself up and kissing him gently. 'I'll marry you, and I'll go with you wherever life takes you, but I have to warn you—I come with eleven pets.'

He laughed. 'I come with four—and life isn't taking us anywhere. Well, not if you'll share your cottage with me and my motley crew. We can extend it, and get it fixed up—hopefully before all the children start arriving. My father wants to retire. He told me that on the phone last night. He's going to sell me his share, and do locum work to cover sick leave and so on. So, you see, we won't have to go anywhere. I'm home for good—for better, for worse— forever.'

He slipped the ring on her finger, and she looked down at it. It was beautiful, a simple square-cut diamond that shone with a quiet brilliance. It swam out of focus, and she swallowed hard and smiled mistily up at him.

'It's beautiful,' she said, choked, and he bent his head.

'Not as beautiful as you,' he said gruffly. 'Nothing could do you justice. I love you.'

'Oh, Andrew, I love you, too,' she said, and drew him down for her kiss.

He was home for good, he said. Home forever.

It sounded perfect.

MILLS & BOON®

Makes any time special™

Mills & Boon publish 29 new titles every month. Select from...

Modern Romance™   Tender Romance™

Sensual Romance™

Medical Romance™ Historical Romance™

MAT2

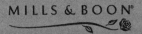

The perfect gift this Christmas from

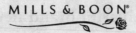

FREE

4 BOOKS
AND A SURPRISE GIFT!

We would like to take this opportunity to thank you for reading this Mills & Boon® book by offering you the chance to take FOUR more specially selected titles from the Medical Romance™ series absolutely FREE! We're also making this offer to introduce you to the benefits of the Reader Service™—

★ FREE home delivery ★ FREE gifts and competitions
★ FREE monthly Newsletter ★ Exclusive Reader Service discounts
★ Books available before they're in the shops

Accepting these FREE books and gift places you under no obligation to buy; you may cancel at any time, even after receiving your free shipment. Simply complete your details below and return the entire page to the address below. *You don't even need a stamp!*

YES! Please send me 4 free Medical Romance books and a surprise gift. I understand that unless you hear from me, I will receive 6 superb new titles every month for just £2.40 each, postage and packing free. I am under no obligation to purchase any books and may cancel my subscription at any time. The free books and gift will be mine to keep in any case.

MOZEC

Ms/Mrs/Miss/Mr ....Initials ....
BLOCK CAPITALS PLEASE

Surname ....

Address ....

....

....Postcode ....

Send this whole page to:
UK: FREEPOST CN81, Croydon, CR9 3WZ
EIRE: PO Box 4546, Kilcock, County Kildare (stamp required)

Offer valid in UK and Eire only and not available to current Reader Service subscribers to this series. We reserve the right to refuse an application and applicants must be aged 18 years or over. Only one application per household. Terms and prices subject to change without notice. Offer expires 30th June 2001. As a result of this application, you may receive further offers from Harlequin Mills & Boon Limited and other carefully selected companies. If you would prefer not to share in this opportunity please write to The Data Manager at the address above.

Mills & Boon® is a registered trademark owned by Harlequin Mills & Boon Limited.
Medical Romance™ is being used as a trademark.